Making Lemonade

Muriel Ellis Pritchett

BLACK ROSE
writing™

The final approval for this literary material is granted by the author.

First printing

This is a work of fiction. Names, characters, businesses, places, events and incidents are either the products of the author's imagination or used in a fictitious manner. Any resemblance to actual persons, living or dead, or actual events is purely coincidental.

ISBN: 978-1-61296-797-4
PUBLISHED BY BLACK ROSE WRITING
www.blackrosewriting.com

Printed in the United States of America
Suggested retail price $16.95

Making Lemonade is printed in Adobe Garamond Pro

This book is dedicated to my always supportive parents, Betty and Ralph Ellis; my high school English teacher, Jane Petty; my fiction writing professor, Dr. Dick O'Brien; and my husband, Harold Pritchett, the techie guru who keeps my computer working and my shoulders massaged.

Special thanks to my dear editor friend and cheerleader, Judy Purdy; to Tuesday Writers Gail Karwoski, Susan Vizurraga and Emma Stephens; and to my favorite art professors, Ted Saupe and Sunkoo Yuh.

Making Lemonade

Chapter One

Happy Birthday, Missouri!

On Missouri Campbell Rothman's fiftieth birthday, she expected her husband Doyle to throw a big, lavish surprise party with her closest friends. She wanted nothing less than some wacky birthday cards, a pile of presents, chocolate cake with fudge frosting and triple chocolate ice cream. Unfortunately, what she got instead was the worst day of her life.

Turning half a century old was a real bitch, Missouri thought, running a comb through her short, curly auburn hair. She examined her face in her rear-view mirror and was relieved to see that overnight she had not turned into a wrinkled old crone. Still, the signs of aging were becoming apparent – the fine lines around her hazel-green eyes, the two creases at the top of her nose and the snugness of her size 18 pants around the waist.

As the light turned green, Missouri moved her foot off the brakes and turned right into the university's North Campus parking deck, only one block from where she worked at the Office of Community Relations. As she lowered her window to insert her key card, the outdoor heat blasted her face. Dang it all, she thought, it was spring, not summer. But she was already sweaty through and through. Was she having another one of those premenopausal hot flashes? The wooden arm rose, and she drove up the ramp of the eight-story deck in search of a parking spot.

She did not see the black SUV until it slammed into her right front fender. Stunned and shaking, she sat in her late model Sentra until a young man peered at her through the driver's window. What a great start to her birthday, she thought. Could this be a bad omen?

"Lady, you all right?" he asked.

Obviously a student, Missouri surmised, noting his jeans, R.E.M. T-shirt and pierced lip. She felt a few trickles of sweat run down her back.

"I'm sorry. I didn't see you." He lowered his face closer to hers. "Are you sure you're okay?"

Missouri nodded. This was her third accident in a campus parking lot in five years. Was there a bull's eye painted somewhere on her car? She sighed loudly. "Nothing's broken." She refrained from screaming out any of the negative words stuck in her throat. She had a feeling that turning fifty and having her car ruined were going to make for a really sucky day.

"I called the campus police, ma'am. Am I glad you're okay."

You and me both, Missouri thought. I didn't want to spend my birthday in the ER.

The young man looked down at her fender. "I don't think you'll be driving this car home."

Exiting her damaged car, Missouri sighed in frustration and dug her cell phone out of her purse. She decided to phone her office – just in case they were planning to surprise her with a birthday brunch or something.

● ● ● ● ●

The tow truck driver said the front axle was bent, and the car probably totaled. The insurance adjuster said it would cost more to fix the car than it was worth. They would send her a check for $4,000.

When Missouri finally walked into her office an hour late, no one wished her happy birthday. No presents, cards or flowers. Just a typical work day. Hoping the accident would not throw a monkey wrench into Doyle's plans for her surprise party, she phoned her husband and asked for a ride home.

"Why do you need a ride? Where's your car?" Doyle asked.

Missouri thought he sounded rather irritated. He probably planned to leave work early to pick up the cake and get the house ready for the party. Thank goodness she had given the house a good cleaning over the weekend. That was what she called planning ahead.

Doyle was not happy to hear about the accident. "$4,000 will not buy you another car."

"At least I wasn't hurt, Doyle. Let's be thankful for that."

The silence on Doyle's end lasted so long Missouri thought they'd been disconnected. "Yes...of course...the most important thing is that you weren't injured."

. . . . .

When Missouri's boss, Vice President William Winslow, called her into his office at the end of the day, she expected him to wish her happy birthday – or at least thank her for staying late four nights in a row to help him with the annual report.

"Missouri, my dear," Winslow greeted her warmly. Too warmly, she thought. Like right before the dentist announces you need a root canal and a new crown.

"Have a seat and let's chat."

Chat? He'd never used that word with her before. Twelve years and they'd never chatted about anything that she could remember. In fact, he'd never been the chatty type. Missouri felt a twist in her stomach. She wondered if she were over-reacting? She forced herself to smile at her distinguished-looking boss, who was retiring in two more weeks after 35 years at the university. He had always reminded her of Cary Grant in his later years. Thick white hair, hardly any wrinkles and a smiling, friendly face. The thought of breaking in Dr. Cooper as the new vice president was daunting, but hopefully he would be glad to have an experienced administrative associate.

"I hear you had a little fender bender this morning," Winslow said.

"Oh yeah, my car's totaled. The SUV that hit me hardly had a scratch."

"University student?"

Missouri nodded.

Winslow flashed a sympathetic fatherly smile. "Don't you worry, my dear. I'm sure that husband of yours will buy you another one. Especially now that he's been appointed to the Gregor Mendel Chair in Genetics."

Missouri raised her eyebrows in surprise at the mention of Doyle's appointment. Her husband, a genetics professor at the university, had failed to mention this to her. He was probably too busy planning her party. Or maybe he was waiting to surprise her. This was a huge deal and it certainly would not have slipped his mind. But Dr. Winslow was right – these appointments came with more money, so Doyle could easily afford to buy her a new car.

"First of all, Missouri, thank you for your many years of hard work, and for all those times you've saved me from roasting myself in some political administrative fire."

Missouri leaned forward, her face flushed with pleasure. "You're so welcome, Dr. Winslow, and you know I've enjoyed working for you, too.

You've been a fair and excellent boss."

Winslow looked down at his hands and sighed. "Thank you, Missouri. That means a lot to me." He coughed slightly. "As you know, Dr. Cooper has been appointed as the new vice president, and he will be taking over this position in two weeks." He paused.

"Don't worry, Dr. Winslow. I'll work just as hard for him as I've worked for you."

"I'm sure you mean that Missouri. However, I talked with Dr. Cooper this morning and he told me that he's bringing his own personal staff with him." He shuffled some papers around on his desk and avoided Missouri's eyes.

His own personal staff? Missouri wasn't sure what this meant for her. Would she have to train them?

Winslow cleared his throat. "That is his prerogative, you know."

Missouri frowned. "I don't understand."

"Dr. Cooper will not need your services." With his fingers, he slid a box of tissues on his desk closer to her.

Missouri was aghast. He wouldn't need her? "Then what am I supposed to do?"

Winslow leaned back in his overstuffed chair and clasped his hands. "We do have some options here, Missouri. I spoke with the dean of the law school at lunch and he has an opening for a senior secretary."

Senior secretary? Missouri's eyes narrowed. That job title was several rungs lower than her present position as administrative associate. Missouri opened her mouth to speak.

Winslow raised his hand. "Wait, I'm not finished. Even though that position is lower than your present position, HR assures me your present salary will continue. And although the dean will not be able to give you a raise next year, HR says that you will be first in line for any position that might open up on campus in the future."

Missouri shook her head furiously. She could not believe the new vice president was rejecting her. After her many years of service and dedication, she was being offered a demotion. She jumped to her feet. "That's unacceptable, Dr. Winslow. I don't want to be a senior secretary."

Winslow nodded sadly and handed her an envelope. "I knew you'd feel that way, Missouri. So I typed up a letter of termination, effective in two weeks. I'm really sorry, my dear. My hands are tied. It's nothing personal." He stood up, walked around his desk and placed his right hand on her shoulder. "You know you are the best administrative associate I've ever had. I really hoped we could find you an equal or better position in another department on campus. Maybe something will open up in the next few months. Let me know and I'll be glad to write you an excellent letter of recommendation." He cleared his throat, again. "Also, you might want to talk this over with Doyle. If you change your mind, let me know."

Her fair and excellent – soon to be former – boss gave her a hug. "I'd love to give you a farewell reception, Missouri. Why don't you set a date, reserve a room at the student center, arrange for a caterer and send out the invitations? Now, my dear, you have a good evening. You deserve it."

Missouri was dismissed. Numbly she walked out of Winslow's office. She couldn't believe it. Here she was...a fifty-year-old work horse...kicked out to pasture...headed for the glue factory. She'd read all those magazine articles. She was half a century old. Nobody would hire her to do anything, except for maybe McDonald's – but the high school kids had cornered the burger-flipping market. Or Wal-Mart – but did the greeters actually get paid? Or Disney World – but no way would Doyle move to Florida.

Could she file a suit for age discrimination? Or would she have to admit she was old? Missouri had not been this angry since Doyle came home with that shiny new red convertible six months ago – after he insisted that she buy a used practical car. After all, he had reminded her, he was entitled to a new car since he was the big breadwinner.

· · · · ·

Doyle stopped his Lexus at the bus stop outside of Missouri's office, and she got in. During their four-mile drive home, very few words were spoken. When Missouri tried to tell Doyle about losing her job, his hands tightened on the steering wheel, and he clinched his jaw.

After one look at his face, she decided to wait until after her party. It wasn't something she wanted to talk about anyway. After all, today was the first day of the rest of her life.

Entering the house ahead of Doyle, Missouri's eyes searched for evidence of a surprise party. She walked into the kitchen. No chocolate birthday cake in sight. She opened the 'fridge. No wine coolers or party food trays. No double-fudge ice cream in the freezer. "Well, dang!" she said. Then she smiled. Maybe Doyle had planned a surprise dinner party downtown?

Doyle came up behind her and grabbed her elbow. "We need to talk."

Missouri followed Doyle into the living room. He must have hidden her present in the entertainment cabinet. Cruise tickets to Tahiti? The thought excited her. She had been dropping hints for over a year now. Had he heard her? "What is it, Doyle?" Missouri asked, sitting down on the brown leather sofa. "Are we going out for dinner?"

"Wha-at?" He looked at her blankly. "Why would you think that?"

"To celebrate my fiftieth birthday, of course."

Doyle made some sort of strangled sound in his throat.

Missouri smiled. Did he really think that would convince her he'd forgotten her big day?

Doyle fell backward into his recliner, burying his face in his hands. "Damn!" He looked up sadly and shook his head side to side wearily. "I'm so sorry, Missouri, I forgot."

Missouri started opening cabinet doors. "Don't tease me, Doyle. Where have you hidden my present?"

"I haven't hidden anything." Doyle rose from the recliner and pulled her down next to him on the sofa.

Missouri studied Doyle carefully, trying to read his face. Was it really possible that he had forgotten her birthday? How could he? Five years earlier, when he'd turned fifty, she gave him a surprise party on campus – complete with a bunch of bananas, an actor in a gorilla suit and a birthday cake. His fellow professors said it was the best surprise party they'd ever attended. Still not accepting the possibility that he had forgotten her birthday, Missouri looked at him hopefully, fully expecting him to pull an envelope from his pocket with plane tickets to Tahiti. Then he would laugh out loud and exclaim "Fooled you!" But the look of angst on Doyle's face finally convinced her that he really had forgotten. She would not be getting a surprise party. No chocolate cake. No trip to Tahiti.

Doyle sighed and rubbed the bridge of his nose wearily. His brown eyes looked solemnly into hers. He cleared his throat. "I don't know how else to tell you this, except to be brutally honest." He paused and swallowed hard. "I want a divorce."

Missouri looked at her husband incomprehensibly. "That's not funny, Doyle. Bad joke!"

"I'm not joking."

She stared at him incredulously. He really wasn't joking. He had forgotten her birthday, and he wanted a divorce. Her eyes widened as shock set in. The truth struck Missouri like a blow to her abdomen. She involuntarily gasped. Her heart pounded in her ears. Shutting her eyes tightly, she covered both ears with her hands and screamed. A long, loud blood-curdling scream.

Doyle's whole body jerked backwards. Then he grabbed her shoulders and shook her until the scream faded into quiet, convulsive sobs. Doyle waited a few moments before releasing his grip. "Missouri? Say something."

"Like what?" She blubbered, the tears flowing from her hazel-green eyes. "I can't believe you would do this to me. Why don't you just grab a kitchen knife, cut out my heart and grind it into hamburger?" She shook her head in disbelief, her auburn curls slinging from side to side.

"Do you have to be so dramatic and emotional? It's not like it's the end of the world, you know. It's only a divorce." Doyle stood up and put his hands in his pocket. "I'm sorry I had to tell you this on your birthday, but it shouldn't come as a surprise, Missouri. You know there really hasn't been a marriage here for years. We're just two ships passing in the night."

Dumbstruck, Missouri opened her mouth to respond, but nothing came out. How could I not have noticed, she wondered, her throat sending out high pitched squeals of agony. Had there been signs that their thirty-two-year-old marriage was in trouble? All those evenings Doyle worked late? Weekend meetings? More and more frequent out-of-town conferences? His lessening interest in sex lately that she had attributed to his age and low testosterone. Between her full-time job and caring for her invalid father-in-law, John Henry, she guessed she had been too tired and too busy to notice.

Doyle's father, a widower in poor health, had moved in with them ten years ago. Their two sons, Michael and Cody, who were in high school at the time, loved their grandfather. Then last year, John Henry's health began to fail. Missouri spent her own personal leave taking her father-in-law to doctor's appointments. She prepared his special meals, saw that he took his medications, and helped him get ready for bed. He died in his sleep six months before her birthday.

Doyle's voice cut through her thoughts. "Missouri, are you listening to me? I've fallen in love with another woman."

Missouri felt an icy numbness spread throughout her body. She suddenly remembered meeting Doyle for the first time – a tall, handsome Navy ensign in his immaculate white uniform. Doyle had introduced himself to her at a reception at the Navy Officer's Club. Three months later, two days after her high school graduation, she and Doyle married in the military chapel.

"Missouri!"

Missouri jumped and blinked open her eyes. "What!?"

Doyle stared back at her apprehensively and concerned. A lock of his graying black hair fell across his perspiring forehead. He combed it back into place with his fingers.

Damn him! He was still good looking. A lump rose in her throat. "Who is she, Doyle?" The question came out soft and strangled. "Is she someone I know?"

Doyle straightened up and slowly walked over to the fireplace, propping his elbow up on the mantle and rubbing the back of his head. He turned his head and glanced back at Missouri, his usual in-control face twitching ever so slightly, his jaw tightening and relaxing.

"Tell me, you son of a bitch!" she screamed.

"Pamelynn Atkins," he responded hoarsely.

Missouri's mind raced into high gear, sorting bits of information, searching for a visual with the name. Suddenly, an image clicked into place – a thin, lanky blonde Britney Spears clone who wore near-nothing tops and hip-hugging, ultra-tight jeans to maximize the exposure of her tanned and toned midriff. A post-doc in Doyle's department.

"Pamelynn Atkins?" Missouri screamed out incredulously. She rose angrily from the sofa and stomped over to Doyle. She tried to slap him across the face, but he grabbed her wrist. "She's young enough to be your daughter, Doyle."

Doyle's neck reddened down into his collar. "Get control of yourself, Missouri. I knew you'd lose it as soon as you found out. That's why I didn't tell you sooner."

"How nice that you finally decided to let me know." Missouri smiled sickeningly. "And just how long have you and little Miss Blondie been getting it on?"

"That's none of your business," he sputtered.

"The hell you say! If it affects our marriage, then it is my business. How long, Doyle?"

"Oh, I don't know...twelve...maybe eighteen months."

"You mean all those months I was taking care of your dad – preparing his special meals, washing his clothes, changing his sheets, driving him to the doctor, waiting on him hand and foot – all that time you were messing around with this girl?"

"Dammit, Missouri, I have needs and I wasn't getting any from you," he spluttered.

"I was working eight hours a day and caring for John Henry. How considerate of you to wait until after your father died to ask for a divorce."

"It was simpler that way, okay? You were so stressed out taking care of Dad, I didn't want to add to it."

"You mean you didn't think Pamelynn would step in as caregiver, and you were afraid your father would disinherit you and give everything to me and your sons."

"I knew it, I knew it! I can't discuss anything with you calmly and sensibly when you go all emotional and crazy on me." He bent over and picked up a black Samsonite carry-on bag from behind the armchair. "I'm moving in with Orson Whitehead for the time being. I'll be back for the rest of my things later. When you get yourself under control, we'll talk more."

Chapter Two

Missouri whimpered as Doyle's red car tore out of the driveway. Her whimper turned into a distressed wail, followed by another blood-curdling scream. In an all-out rage, she swept a pile of Doyle's books and magazines off the coffee table. "I hate you!" She threw every single sofa pillow across the floor and jumped up and down on all of them. Then she grabbed a white porcelain lamp off the end table and lifted it over her head. Before she could smash it on the floor, she remembered it was a Christmas present from her favorite Aunt Leekie. The same aunt who at their engagement party announced after three glasses of champagne that Doyle was just a little bit off and might not be good marriage material.

Returning the lamp to the end table, Missouri's eyes locked on the plastic model of the USS Eisenhower that had taken Doyle months to assemble, glue together and paint. With a sinister grin, she snatched it off the book shelf and threw it against the brick hearth. Not satisfied to see it broken into three pieces, she ground her heels into each piece, screaming "Take that you asshole" with every crunch of plastic.

Huffing and puffing from her tirade, Missouri fell onto the sofa, screaming until she was exhausted and unable to cry any more.

• • • • •

When the phone rang, Missouri almost didn't pick up. She didn't want to talk to anyone. But after checking the caller ID, she saw it was her oldest son Michael, who was in the Air Force and stationed in Japan. She knew it was early the next morning there. Michael was probably calling to wish her happy birthday before he headed off to work.

Missouri lifted the phone to her ear. "Hello, Michael." She hoped he couldn't hear any stress or hysteria in her voice. No need to upset him, when he was on the other side of the world and couldn't do anything to help.

"Mom?" He hesitated briefly. "Are you okay?"

Missouri inhaled sharply. Did he know? "I appreciate your concern, Michael, but turning 50 isn't the end of the world. I don't feel any different than I did when I was 49."

"What? Oh...that's not..." Dead air. Missouri could almost hear his brain processing. "Today's your birthday?"

"Isn't that why you called? To wish me happy 50th birthday. It is a major milestone in my life." *That and having your dad ask for a divorce so he can marry some young, tight-ass little slut.*

"No, but...I mean...Ye-es, of course, Mom...uh...Happy Birthday. I can't believe you're fifty years old."

"Neither can I, Michael. Look, Sweetheart, I know this phone call is costing you. Thanks for the birthday wishes. Please give my love to Lizzie."

"Mom, wait! Don't hang up. I'm not finished."

Of course not, Missouri thought. He obviously heard from Doyle and felt obligated to call.

"Mom, Dad just emailed me that you guys are getting divorced. What happened? I didn't realize you guys were having problems."

Missouri pictured her son on the other end of the line in his Air Force uniform. Like his dad, Michael loved airplanes, boats and all sports. His wife Lizzie loved everything he loved. After eight years of marriage, they had produced no grandchildren for her to love and spoil. Missouri had long since buried any idea of becoming a grandmother. What good would it be to have grandchildren living on the other side of the world?

"Neither did I, Michael." Missouri carried her cell phone out on the deck and sat in the swing. It was early May and the trees had maxed out their green foliage. Most of the flowers had bloomed out. Only a lone yellow rose withered at the end of its stem. *Just like me,* she thought

"Dad said you never go out socially any more, you never talk to each other, and you aren't even sleeping together."

That Doyle had shared such intimate details with their son infuriated and sickened Missouri. "Your father snores loudly, Michael. He suggested I move into your brother's old room so I could get some sleep. And we never go out together or communicate because your father is always working or going to conferences."

"Maybe you should have gone with him to those meetings..."

Missouri could feel the beginning of a migraine right between her eyes.

"First of all, Michael, your father never asked me to go with him and secondly, someone had to stay home to take care of your grandfather. Is there anything else you want to know?" She knew she sounded quite irritated on her end. Which she was, because Pamelynn never missed going to a single conference with Doyle.

"Don't jump down my throat, Mom. I just don't understand what you did to push Dad away. Why would you want to throw away thirty-two years of marriage?"

Michael's words burned into her brain. Was it true, she wondered? Had she been the one to push Doyle away? Missouri considered telling Michael about Pamelynn, but she couldn't do it. She didn't want to admit out loud that Doyle was replacing her with a sweet young thing. Maybe Doyle was having a midlife crisis and just needed some space and time. "Michael, if you figure it out, please let me know. Thanks for calling. Tell Lizzie hello. Love you!" Then she disconnected before her hysterics returned.

Missouri hung up and sighed. She continued to sit, swinging back and forth ever so slightly. The gentle motion hypnotized her and she became oblivious to time and her surroundings. Suddenly she was jarred back to the living by shouting and a loud pounding on the front door. Missouri jumped up and ran into the house. She turned on the outside porch light and opened the heavy oak door. Her youngest son Cody stood on the front steps.

"Mom, where were you? You scared me to death!" he blurted out. "I called you, but the phone was busy, so I drove home to check on you. When you didn't come to the door right away, I thought you were...uh...might have...uh...thought about...uh..."

"So your father called you, too?" Missouri was not surprised. Even though Cody lived in Atlanta, it was over a one-hour drive for him to come home. Doyle obviously wanted to spin this divorce issue to his advantage.

Cody rubbed the back of his neck. "Mmmm, maybe."

Missouri sighed loudly. "What, Cody? What did you think? That I slit my wrists and was lying on the floor in a pool of blood? Or drowned myself in the bathtub?" Cody blushed and Missouri knew that was exactly what he thought. She reached up and brushed a tendril of dark curly hair off his forehead.

While Michael was a chip off his father's block in looks and personality, Cody was a Missouri clone. Where Doyle and Michael were athletic, logical, analytical, serious, and left-brained, Cody was arty, intuitive, full of personality and all right-brained. He favored Missouri with reddish highlights in his hair and hazel eyes that changed to green or blue when he wore the right color shirt or jacket.

"Let me guess," she said softly. "Your father called and suggested you drop over for a visit since he was dumping me for a woman young enough to be your sister?"

Cody nodded and swallowed hard. "I...uh...I...uh..." His eyes watered and he unobtrusively brushed away a tear that rolled out of a corner of his right eye.

Missouri put her arms around him and he hugged her back. They stood holding each other for several minutes, with Missouri sobbing loudly and inconsolably, Cody quietly shedding a few tears of his own. "I don't know what I'm going to do," she cried.

When Missouri pulled away from Cody, he fumbled and pulled a handkerchief from his back pocket. Wiping her eyes with it, Missouri walked into the den and settled into the brown leather sofa that Doyle insisted was necessary for the perfect guy room with dark oak panels and testosterone state-of-the-art electronics, including surround-sound, wall-mounted HDTV, the newest Blu-ray DVD player, and a TiVo that did everything except serve up bourbon and branch.

Cody sat down beside her and took her hands in his. "Mom, I came home because I love you, and I think Dad is being a real jerk. I don't understand why he's doing this. Maybe he's having a midlife crisis."

Missouri smiled at her sensitive son – writer, editor and peacemaker. After graduating from the journalism college at the university, he took a job as an assistant editor for a small magazine in Atlanta. He shared a small two-bedroom apartment in Midtown and rode MARTA to work. Outside of his job, he wrote poetry. Since college, he had won several literary awards for his efforts and was working on his Great American Novel.

"I don't have any answers, Cody. I didn't see this coming. It was a complete shock for me."

"Remember the year I finished high school and left for college? You and Dad had several friends go through divorces."

Missouri nodded. "How could I forget?" Missouri and Doyle knew three couples who divorced after more than 25 years of marriage. When their children left the "nest," the couples felt like they were living with strangers. Two of the couples, who went through counseling, rediscovered each other and remarried. Missouri didn't understand why Doyle was so unhappy now when they had managed to survive the "empty nest." Was it because their "nest" wasn't officially empty until Doyle's father died?

Cody reached out and shook Missouri's shoulder gently. "Mom? Mom, are you all right?"

Missouri jumped. Her eyes focused on Cody's. "What? Oh, I'm sorry, Cody. I was thinking about our friends who went through those terrible divorces."

"That's what I was saying. Sure, they went and got divorced, but some of them remarried, remember? Maybe you and Dad just need some counseling and time apart to realize you really love each other."

Missouri shook her head. "That's a nice thought, Cody, but none of our friends who divorced were in love with someone else."

"I don't think Dad really loves her. He's feeling old and he's attracted to her youthfulness and energy."

"Yeah, her youthfulness. And don't forget her breasts haven't fallen to her navel, her face isn't sagging, her belly doesn't need a girdle to hold it in, her short-term memory is still functioning at a high level and she doesn't have to spend half an hour each day brushing, flossing and rinsing to save her teeth and another half hour applying industrial strength moisturizers and firming creams to fight the wrinkles and dry skin."

"She's gotta be twenty years younger than Dad," Cody said. "At some point, she'll realize Dad is older than dirt. What could they possibly have in common? Can you see Dad going downtown with her to drink beer and listen to some new hot rock band? Or her going to Atlanta to see a production of a Wagner or Puccini opera? One day she'll leave him for a cute, young guy like me," he said, with just a hint of a smile on his lips and a tug on the diamond earring in his right ear.

Missouri looked at her son's earring and was reminded of the evening Cody came home with his ear pierced. If John Henry had not stepped in between the two angry, shouting males, Doyle would have kicked Cody out of the house.

"Boys will be boys," John Henry told Doyle and gently reminded him of his own indiscretions during high school – smoking marijuana in the garage, "borrowing" the family car at the age of 14 and losing his virginity to an older cousin in his parents' bed while his sister's wedding reception was going on downstairs.

Missouri half-smiled. "Life can be so cruel and unfair. This has been one hell of a day." Slowly – and somewhat calmly – she told him about totaling her car and losing her job.

Cody leaned back and put his arm around Missouri's shoulders and squeezed. "Mom, all my life, you've told me life isn't fair – that you have to accept the lemons life tosses you and make lemonade."

"Where are you going with this, Cody?"

"That Dad's leaving, totaling your car and losing your job are your lemons. What can you do to make lemonade out of that?"

Missouri looked at her son in astonishment. Make lemonade out of lemons? She couldn't believe that her son was tossing her own motherly advice back to her. "But these aren't lemons being thrown at me. We're talking about nuclear bombs. Total annihilation of life as I know it, as our family knows it. Can't you see that?" Her voice caught and she ran outside on the deck. Standing at the railing, she gulped down deep breaths and fought for control of her emotions.

Cody came up behind her and placed his hands on her shoulders. "I'm sorry Dad has hurt all of us so deeply, especially you. I wish I could wave a magic wand and make everything better. Want me to talk to Pamelynn? Maybe she doesn't realize what Dad looks like in a swimsuit. Or that he snores so loud, nobody can get any sleep. Or that he's always right, even when he's wrong. Or that he's stubborn and wants everything done his way."

Missouri shook her head. "No, Cody, I want you to stay as far away from her as you can. Promise?" The last thing Missouri wanted was to be the bitter, angry ex-wife.

"Sure thing, Mom. Whatever you want me to do – as long as I agree, of course."

"Cody!"

Cody grinned sheepishly. "Okay, Mom. Let me get my things out of the car."

"What things?"

"I'm spending the weekend with you to celebrate your birthday."

"Cody, it's Thursday. Don't you have to work tomorrow?" Although Missouri loved it when Cody came home, she didn't want him to be here for a suicide watch.

"Not a problem. I took tomorrow off. Told the editor I needed to go home to celebrate my mom's 50th birthday."

"You shouldn't use your vacation time to babysit me."

"Mom, I love coming home. Where else can I get three hot meals a day prepared by a woman who loves me? Besides, I have lots of dirty clothes that need washing. I'm here, I'm staying, I'm not leaving you here alone on your birthday. Tonight, I'm cooking Italian." He kissed fingers to the air and ran his thumb along Missouri's cheek. "Mama Mia, the meal I have planned for you!"

Chapter Three

Cody's Italian dinner was *delizioso*. He served prosciutto and melon for the antipasto course, bread soup for the second course, shrimp risotto and asparagus for the main course, and tiramisu for dessert. And even though her world had just caved in, Missouri surprisingly found comfort in her son's company and his cooking. After dinner, they retired to the deck swing with their *caffè latte*.

While they sipped their coffee in silence, Missouri tried to pinpoint where her marriage took a wrong turn. Did she and Doyle marry too young? Actually, she was kind of old compared to others in her family. Her mother had been sixteen and still in high school. If it hadn't been for the draft, her parents might have waited longer to marry. Her maternal grandmother had been fifteen. Her grandfather, who was ten years older and weary from years of working as a merchant marine, returned home – ready to settle down and start a family. Nobody in her family had ever divorced.

Things were just starting to heat up in the Persian Gulf when Doyle and Missouri were married. His first duty station was Oceana Naval Base in Norfolk. Michael was born at the Naval Hospital in Portsmouth a little more than two years after they married. Up until his birth, Missouri and Doyle led an idyllic life with warm sunny weekend days on Virginia Beach, evenings of parties, crabbing in the tidal creeks, and sailing around Chesapeake Bay. With a baby to care for, their social life became somewhat complicated, but not impossible once they found a good babysitter.

A year after Michael was born, Doyle received orders to the U.S. Naval Support Activity in Naples, Italy. Their sponsor had their base living quarters ready for them the day they arrived in Naples. While Doyle – recently promoted to lieutenant – was at work, Missouri would put Michael in his buggy and go exploring off-base.

During one day of exploration, she found a small *belle arti* store down a quiet *vicolo* and went inside. Missouri was delighted to find a large variety of brushes, watercolors and paper. Using money she had been saving for a pair of black leather shoes, Missouri purchased a small set of watercolor pans, two brushes and a pad of watercolor paper. That same afternoon she sketched and painted in a nearby park. Doyle laughed at her finished paintings and said she was wasting her time.

Two years after their second son Cody was born, the family left Naples for the Norfolk Naval Shipyard, where Doyle was assigned to an aircraft carrier, the USS John F. Kennedy. After being deployed three times to the Mediterranean, Doyle walked away from military life and straight into graduate studies at the University of Michigan.

The G.I. Bill paid for everything, and the family lived in married housing. After receiving his master's degree in genetics, Doyle was accepted into the PhD program at Stanford. Throughout these years, Missouri looked after Michael and Cody, helped them with their homework, carpooled them to after-school activities, took them to the doctor when they were sick and kept them from disturbing Doyle while he studied. Occasionally, when Doyle wasn't around, she pulled out her watercolors.

Finally, Doyle graduated with honors and accepted an assistant professor position in genetics at the University of Georgia. When Missouri approached Doyle about going to college herself, he laughed. "You don't need a college degree," he explained. "You have an MRS degree. I'll take care of you." And over the years he had.

• • • • •

The next morning, while Cody was cooking bacon and whole wheat blueberry pancakes for breakfast, Doyle unlocked the front door and walked in. "What are you doing home?" he asked Missouri, who was sitting at the table drinking coffee. "Did you call in sick or take the day off?"

Missouri, whose back was to the door, didn't bother to turn around. "I lost my job."

"What the hell? How did you manage that?" Doyle asked, walking around the table to face her.

She stared at Doyle in silence. It thoroughly irritated Missouri that he assumed she'd done something wrong to lose her job. "I didn't do anything wrong." She tried to remain calm, when all she wanted to do was slap his face until it turned purple. Maybe even leave some claw marks on his cheek. "For your information, the new vice president is bringing his own staff and does not want me."

Doyle spluttered. "Are you telling me they didn't offer you another position?" he asked, pouring himself a cup of coffee. "Hmmm, excellent coffee, son," he turned to face Cody. "Glad you could come over and stay with your mother last night." Doyle looked back at Missouri, who had not responded to his question. "Well?"

"Yes, they offered me a position as a senior secretary in the law school, which I immediately turned down."

"Are you crazy, woman? Why would you do something idiotic like that?" he asked glaring at her. Missouri pursed her lips and refused to answer.

Cody touched his father's arm. "Dad, Mom didn't want to take a demotion and do secretarial work."

"At least it would have been a job. Now you have no paycheck."

Missouri looked down at her hands. "Unemployment."

"That's hardly anything and it won't last forever. Dammit, woman, you're 50 years old. Don't you realize how difficult it is for old women to find decent-paying jobs. Maybe it's not too late to accept that secretarial position. Let me call the dean."

"No!" Missouri shouted. "I don't want the job!"

A red flush crept up Doyle's neck and across his face. Missouri knew she should speak carefully and not fuel his anger fire, but she didn't care one bit about his blood pressure. Pamelynn could worry about that now. Her eyes narrowed as their eyes locked. "No paycheck, Doyle? That's what this is all about, isn't it? If my unemployment runs out and I don't have a job, you might have to support me?"

Doyle banged his coffee mug down on the granite counter top so hard, coffee sloshed everywhere. "Do you see, Cody? Your mother makes it impossible to have any kind of a pleasant conversation with her. I'm only here to pack the rest of my things." He walked briskly out of the kitchen without a backward glance.

"I didn't know Dad could be such a total jerk." Cody sighed and handed his mother his handkerchief.

Missouri wiped away tears of anger and frustration. "Cody, I need a lawyer."

"That's a wise decision." Cody grabbed his laptop and Googled local attorneys. He pushed his computer across the counter to Missouri. She scanned the list of attorneys specializing in personal injuries, disability law, debt relief,

DUI accidents, medical malpractice and wrongful death. She passed up large law firms and focused on a two-lawyer practice specializing in child custody and divorce cases with costs starting at $199. One quick call and she had an appointment before lunch.

• • • • •

Missouri was amazed at how fast one could get an uncontested divorce in Georgia. Once Doyle turned down marriage counseling and Missouri accepted the inevitability of the divorce, it was just a matter of dividing property and making concessions. Doyle was very generous in the settlement proceedings. Probably due to a lot of guilt on his part, especially after her attorney pointed out to the judge how Missouri had spent many years as primary caregiver for Doyle's father.

In addition to the house and a cash settlement, Missouri was given money to purchase a used car, which Doyle said would last ten more years if she kept it serviced on a regular basis. After much arguing between lawyers and input from the judge, it was agreed that Doyle would pay for Missouri to go to college and get a degree.

"After all, Dr. Rothman, you married her out of high school before she had a chance at any higher education." The judge leaned forward and peered over his half-frame glasses at Doyle. "She bore you two sons and took care of you for thirty-two years and your own father as well for more than ten." The judge paused, his bushy brows scrunched together in a frown across the bridge of his nose. "If you're going to dump her now for a younger woman, then I think you can pay her way through college so she can get a better job to support herself. Don't you agree?"

An angry, but intimidated Doyle shrank back into his chair and nodded in agreement. The judge banged his gavel and waddled his large ample-robed body out of the courtroom.

Cold, trembling and weak, Missouri blinked back tears. It's over, she thought. My life as I know it is over.

Missouri's young lawyer, two years out of law school, turned to face her and smiled. "Well, I guess this wraps it up, Mrs. Rothman. You have a happy life, you hear?" He extended his pudgy right hand toward her. Numb from the proceedings and in shock, she allowed him to shake her hand. His handshake was soft and limp. Nondescript. Blah. Just like her life.

"Have a 'happy life'? Is that all you have to say?" Missouri's whole body shook in anger and sorrow. She forced herself to stand and face her lawyer, whose smile was now frozen on his face. "Let me tell you what kind of happy life I'm having after being dumped by my husband, so he can marry a cute, bouncy blonde with perky boobs and an 18-inch waist. Our closest married friends are ostracizing me and sidling over to the new couple's front door. My so-called best friends are suddenly too busy for lunch or long talks.

"My life, which has been devoted to raising children, being a supportive wife and caring for an invalid father-in-law, is now a shattered nightmare. I've lost my husband, my job, my friends, my self-esteem – my entire life. And now you – my own lawyer – smiles and tells me to go have a 'happy life.' How the hell am I supposed to do that?"

Chapter Four

Cody continued to drive home from Atlanta every weekend. Missouri suspected his father and brother Michael encouraged him to do this. After all, who knew what an emotional, hysterical old woman in a divorced-depressed, premenopausal condition could do to herself. But she didn't allow herself to question Cody's motives, since she was always happy to spend time with her baby boy.

Cody spent his weekends at home working on his laptop at the patio table. Missouri usually sat in the swing, holding a cup of cold coffee and staring at nothing. Her thoughts always wandered down the same road. Where had the marriage gone wrong? How could she have prevented it? What was she going to do now?

Her efforts to find a job at her age, and with her lack of education, had so far proven fruitless. Her one job offer had been as a receptionist in a doctor's office for less than half of what she'd been getting at the university. Doyle was right, she decided. She was just plain stupid not to have taken that secretarial job at the law school. Who else would hire such an old, fat, ugly loser as herself?

"Mom!" Cody's voice sounded in Missouri's ear, interrupting her thoughts.

Missouri jumped, startled out of her private pity party. "What?" She sat up straight in the swing, nearly dropping her coffee cup. Only then did she notice the willowy ash-brown blonde with a cane standing beside Cody. "Oh, my gosh," she exclaimed, jumping to her feet and giving her old high school chum a big hug. "Is it really you, Amelia? Such a pleasant surprise!" She stepped back and looked at her friend. "When did you get into town? Why didn't you call to tell me you were coming?"

Amelia smiled and clasped Missouri's hands. "This was a last-minute decision on my part. I heard about you and Doyle through the grapevine and decided to rush out to see you."

"I'm so glad you did. How long can you stay?" Missouri glanced over at Cody and noticed he was holding a red overnight bag and avoiding eye contact with her. "And which grapevine did you hear this from, Amelia?" she asked, looking straight at Cody's face.

"Oh, the little birdie grapevine," Amelia replied vaguely, yet pleasantly.

"I see. This explains why Cody bought three pork chops for dinner tonight."

Amelia chuckled and put her arm around a flustered Cody. "You're a good son, Cody." As she kissed him on the cheek, he wriggled out of her grasp.

"Why don't I take Amelia's bag to the guest room and get a start on some lunch while you two catch up?" Cody disappeared into the house.

The two friends hugged each other again, laughed and sat in the swing. "I can't believe you traveled all the way from Los Angeles to visit me."

"Hey! Weren't we best buds in high school?"

"Best buds until I married Doyle and left Athens to see the world."

"And I married Lt. Maxwell Carpenter for the same reason."

"But I returned to Athens to settle down and you didn't," Missouri reminded Amelia. After Max retired from the Navy, he moved his family to San Diego, where he accepted an upper management position with a large corporation. "We used to see each other when you came home for the holidays, but after your parents died, you didn't come back to Georgia."

"I know, but we do catch up in our Christmas newsletters."

"We're friends on Facebook," Missouri said.

"Yes, but when was the last time we chatted online?"

Missouri shrugged and smiled. "Forever. I don't even do email anymore. Between my job and taking care of John Henry, I didn't have time for social networking."

Amelia patted Missouri's hand. "But your father-in-law is gone now, and we're still best friends. We support each other through good times and bad."

Missouri nodded, remembering how five years earlier, Amelia had become completely bedridden with rheumatoid arthritis and suffered acute depression. Max, who apparently wasn't cut out to be a caregiver, left her in the care of her sister in Los Angeles and divorced her. A year later, a new miracle drug on the market for arthritis, plus cutting-edge surgery, gave Amelia her life back.

"Amelia, you look really good," Missouri said. "The last time I saw you, I thought you'd never get out of bed, again, much less walk through my front door."

"That makes two of us, Sweetie! I never thought I'd be able to stand, again, much less walk. Yet, here I am – a walking miracle, according to my rheumatologist." Amelia leaned back into the swing. "This feels good to sit here in the sun and relax." She shut her eyes, but kept speaking. "Is that what you're doing in this swing, Missouri, relaxing? Or were you feeling sorry for yourself?"

Missouri closed her eyes as two tears rolled down her cheeks. She wiped them away quickly. "I'm sorry, Amelia. Sometimes I just can't hold it back." She spoke softly, trying to swallow the lump in her throat.

"Then don't hold back. Getting divorced and losing your job are both high stressors. Too much stress can kill you. You should scream, tear your clothes, throw things, break stuff – especially if it belongs to Doyle." Amelia grinned at Missouri. "But you can't continue this pity party indefinitely."

"What are you saying?"

"Look at yourself, Missouri. You're drowning in a sea of despair. That's why I'm here with the life preserver. Cody asked me to help you make lemonade."

Missouri threw back her head and hooted. Then she laughed until her sides ached and she cried hysterically. Amelia reached into a large red Gucci bag and pulled out a handful of tissue, shooing a concerned Cody back into the house. She moved over and sat down beside Missouri, her right arm around her shoulders, her left hand distributing tissues. After a few minutes, the convulsive sobs and tears ended, and Missouri wiped her eyes and blew her nose on the last of the tissues.

"That's a good job, Missouri. Now let's declare the pity party is over. It's time for you to get on with the rest of your life."

"But how do I do that?" Missouri asked. "I feel like I'm in a speeding car going downhill. The brakes and the steering wheel don't work, and I'm too scared to open the door and jump out."

"Your friends will help you through this."

"Yeah, right. That's a crock. My so-called friends are currently hanging out with Doyle and his new honey Pamelynn. Michael is off on the other side of the world and poor Cody has his own life in Atlanta. I have no one," she whispered, her voice tapering off.

"You have me," said Amelia. "I've been in your shoes and I'm not going to let you mope around and feel sorry for yourself. Now listen up, because I'm only telling you this once."

Missouri turned toward her high school chum. "I'm a lost cause, Amelia. I'm a fat, stupid old woman who can't find a good job." Then Missouri wished she'd kept her mouth shut as she remembered what Amelia had gone through. "I'm sorry." She sat up straight. "I have my health, a roof over my head, food on the table and a car that runs. What I don't have is control over my life, and I don't know how to get that."

Amelia shook her head. "Missouri, I know you won't believe this, but you are a much stronger person than you think you are. You've raised two sons almost singlehandedly because Doyle was too busy with his career. Then you kept Doyle's dad alive and happy for a long, long time. You've done your duty. It's time for the Missouri Campbell I remember from high school to start looking out for number one. It's time for you to live out your fantasies and put your needs ahead of everyone else's."

"Fantasies? Me? You've got to be kidding!" Missouri considered herself too old to live any fantasies.

"Yes, Missouri, fantasies. You and I both had our fantasies in high school. Think back to our senior year."

"I'm too old and senile to remember that far back."

"Either play along with me or I'll hit you with my cane." Amelia lifted her cane.

Missouri closed her eyes. "Okay, okay, let me see...our senior year...we cut 6th period a lot."

"Because you said Latin class put you to sleep."

Missouri relaxed and took a deep breath, thinking about senior year. "I remember human biology class."

"Yes, the baby pigs we had to dissect." Even after all these years, Missouri blushed at the memory. "Is it my fault undeveloped testicles looked like a vagina to me?"

Both friends laughed boisterously. "What about the quarter we studied blood?" prompted Amelia. "We pricked our fingers and looked at our blood under the microscope."

"Don't remind me. I remember looking at my blood and squealing, 'It's moving!'"

"Oh Lordy me, do I ever remember that!" exclaimed Amelia. "Mrs. White looked over her glasses, straight down her nose at you and said, "I certainly hope so, Miss Campbell, otherwise, you'd be dead."

"What about all those evening road trips?" Missouri asked, getting off the subject of human biology class. "We'd hop in that clunker you called a car."

"Hey! It was an old Datsun and I don't remember you complaining about the transportation back then."

"No, not at all. It got us to all the games and social events. It was a good ride and we had some great times."

"Yes, we really did," said Amelia and sighed contentedly. "We were the 'bestest' of buddies. Remember lying around on your living room floor after school and imagining what we would be doing when we grew up?"

"Vaguely." Missouri cringed.

Amelia reached over and poked Missouri with her cane.

"Ouch...okay...It's coming back. I wanted to find a man, get married and have babies."

"Can you believe that becoming wives and mothers was that important to us? We were so naïve and clueless," Amelia said.

They laughed out loud. "It does sound ridiculous now that I think about it," Missouri said.

They laughed louder. "I'm so glad you came to see me, Amelia. I didn't think I would ever find anything to laugh about, again."

"You're going to find more to laugh about because I remember that you wanted to be an artist. I still have the caricature you did of me," said Amelia, reaching into her Gucci bag and producing a folded piece of yellowed drawing paper. She handed it to Missouri who carefully unfolded it and looked at the graphite drawing.

"I can't believe you still have this. I did lots of these for everyone." Missouri remembered drawing caricatures of her fellow classmates and teachers on everything from napkins and paper bags to good drawing paper. She truly enjoyed doing that.

"Mrs. Coley said you were the most talented student in her class, remember? You were amazing."

"Yes, art was my favorite class. I wanted to go to the university and major in art and you wanted to major in music and become a concert pianist. What happened to our dreams, Amelia?"

"They were forgotten when we met two good-looking sailors and went down different paths," Amelia said, her voice turning serious. "With my arthritic hands, I can't follow my dream. But you can still follow yours. As much as you loved art, why didn't you continue to draw?"

Missouri sighed. "I actually did a little bit of watercolor and loved it, but by the time the boys were born, I had no time and no energy. Doyle always thought it was a foolish pastime anyway."

Amelia folded up the drawing and put it back in her bag. "Cody says your divorce settlement includes money for education?"

"My lawyer said that in today's job market and because of my age, I should take classes at the technical school to learn new skills or get a college degree. A degree would help me get a better job than serving up fries at a fast food place or answering the phone in a doctor's office."

Amelia gently punched Missouri's shoulder. "Here's your chance. Enroll in art school at the university and follow your dream?"

Missouri made a face. "At my age, Amelia? That is laughable. I would be older than the teachers." Older than dirt, she thought.

"But the money for education and job training is there. Doyle has to pay for it." She leaned toward Missouri and lowered her voice conspiratorially. "Look at it as money he won't have available to spend on a new wife. You do know how much it costs these days to attend the university?" Amelia asked shrewdly.

The corners of Missouri's mouth turned up briefly, but settled into a frown. "I don't know, Amelia. I doubt seriously if I could get accepted into the university."

Amelia reached into her Gucci bag and pulled out some papers. "First thing you do is apply for admission to UGA. It's all online now. Cody and I will help you do it tonight."

Missouri reached out her hand to protest, but Amelia waved it away. "Special arrangements can be made about taking the SAT, again, if necessary. But you scored well in high school. You were a National Merit winner, remember? You graduated in the top of your class and you had already been accepted at the university and awarded a scholarship. I don't see any problem with you getting admitted."

Missouri shifted her jaw as she considered the possibility. "Even if I can get into the university, they are very picky about who they let into the art school. You have to have all sorts of recommendations, plus an awesome portfolio," Missouri explained.

Amelia huffed. "Missouri, no excuses. Tomorrow you're going to visit your old art teacher, Mrs. Coley. Here's her phone number." Amelia handed her a piece of paper. "Tonight we're going to dig up work for a portfolio. What do you say?"

Blinking back tears, Missouri smiled jubilantly and pulled Amelia to her feet. "You're the best girlfriend a person could have."

Chapter Five

Missouri looked at the boxes she had pulled out of the closet in her office/work room. Several dated back to high school and beyond. Her mother, bless her soul, had boxed up everything after Missouri and Doyle married. From one partially crushed corrugated cardboard box, Missouri pulled out her moth-eaten lettered drill team sweater and a book of pressed corsages from high school dances. She found old pom-poms from football and basketball games, a scrapbook of memories, old annuals, brittle copies of the school paper, and finally, in the very bottom of one box, a moldy black portfolio.

Loosening the ties on the top and sides, Missouri opened the portfolio on the floor and carefully pulled out watercolors, and drawings in pastels, charcoal and pencil. She spread the artwork across her bed and stepped back to view them.

"What do you think, Amelia?"

Her old friend picked up a charcoal portrait drawing of their American history teacher in high school and a watercolor of the University of Georgia Arch on North Campus with downtown restaurants and shops in the background.

Amelia licked her bottom lip thoughtfully. "Missouri, they're much better than I remembered. Honey, they're damn good."

•   •   •   •   •

Not only did Thelma Coley remember Missouri, but she sounded quite pleased to hear from her former student. "Goodness gracious, child. I always had high hopes that one day you'd make it to art school. I'm so proud of you for applying to the university. Why don't you come over for tea this afternoon at 2 o'clock and bring your artwork? I can't wait to lay these old feeble eyes on you."

Missouri dropped the receiver into the cradle and smiled happily at Amelia. "She remembers me! And she wants to see me."

Amelia thumped her cane on the floor. "And you're surprised?" Missouri nodded. "Then it's a good thing you're going to see her. Maybe she'll be able to boost your sagging self-confidence."

"You're coming with me, aren't you?"

"First of all, your teacher wants to see you, not Amelia who couldn't draw a line without a ruler. Secondly, I promised my cousins I'd spend some time with them while I'm in town."

"Dang it!" complained Missouri.

Amelia chuckled. "I haven't heard that exclamation from you since high school. Some things never change. But before I leave, we need to talk about you making some changes for the better."

Missouri frowned. "Changes? Why? What sort of changes?"

"Just what I said, 'changes for the better.' Changes to boost your morale and self-esteem."

Missouri's eyes narrowed. "Only two things would boost my morale and self-esteem – getting a good job with a big salary and having Pamelynn dump Doyle for a man her own age."

· · · · ·

Cody didn't look up from his laptop when his mom and Amelia headed for the YWCO to sign up for classes in body sculpting, aerobics and Pilates. Amelia also insisted that Missouri hire a personal trainer to help get her into shape.

From the Y, they had an appointment with a diet nutrition specialist, who talked to Missouri about eating better and healthier, and losing weight. The thirty-something diet nutrition specialist did not have an ounce of fat to pinch. "How much do you weigh, Mrs. Rothman?"

Missouri sighed. "Let's just say I'm fifty pounds heavier than I was in high school," she admitted reluctantly. "But I'm a healthy, fat person."

The not-an-ounce-of-fat-to-pinch nutritionist grinned. "Yes, Mrs. Rothman, you are not obese, but if you don't start right now making healthier food choices, you could become obese in a few more years. How is your cholesterol and blood pressure?"

Missouri squirmed in her seat. "I'm taking statin to lower my cholesterol."

"If you can lose weight, it will lower your cholesterol and blood pressure, and put you at lower risk for diabetes, heart disease and strokes."

"Not to mention looking more attractive to the opposite sex," pointed out

Amelia.

Missouri's cheeks turned pink. "Amelia! I'm a divorced older woman, not some desperate unmarried thirty-something looking for romance and sex." After being royally screwed over and burned by Doyle, the last thing Missouri wanted to do was get involved with another man.

"Being more attractive will give you – the older, jobless woman – an edge in the job market." Amelia patted Missouri's hand. "Think about it."

Bitterly remembering her recent job rejections, Missouri decided there was some validity in what Amelia was saying. She let out a long breath. "Okay, I see how being more attractive is not a bad thing." She looked at the nutritionist who was looking amused by the conversation between Missouri and Amelia. "So give me the bad news. Will I have to give up my wine, beer and Dove Bars to lose a few pounds?"

· · · · ·

After lunch at the Last Resort downtown, Amelia insisted that Missouri go to a popular salon in the Five Points area for a new flattering haircut and styling. In the past, between her work schedule and caring for her father-in-law, Missouri rarely found time for a haircut, beyond trimming the ends every few months at Billie Jean's Great Cuts. She merely pulled back her thick, curly, unmanageable auburn hair and tied it at the nape of her neck.

As hairdresser Jean Paul untied the ribbon, Missouri's curls exploded down to her shoulders. Jean Paul picked up a clump of tight frizzy curls. "Lots of people would die for these curls," he said with a heavy French accent. "Do you want the ends trimmed? Or could I do something more creative? What do you think?"

"I'm not sure." Missouri felt uncomfortable at the thought of change.

"The correct answer is 'Oui, Jean Paul, I need a creative hairstyle to go with my new exciting lifestyle,'" piped in Amelia.

"But Doyle doesn't like my hair short."

Amelia shoved Missouri. "Listen to yourself. Doyle left you for a younger woman. What do you care what he thinks? I say cut it off!"

Jean Paul looked to Missouri for confirmation. As she nodded apprehensively, Jean Paul's thin lips parted into an ear-to-ear grin. *"Ma cheri,* let's do it! Jean Paul will make a new woman out of you!"

. . . . .

Missouri parked her new used car in front of Thelma Coley's home and peered at Jean Paul's creation in the rearview mirror. She felt like a big chunk of herself had disappeared. Special de-frizzing shampoo and conditioner, and a just-below-the-ears-length cut had removed any unruliness – leaving Missouri with an attractive, well-tamed look. Jean Paul threw in a free facial, a little mascara and lipstick.

When Cody first saw his mom, his look of amazement had been priceless. "Whoa, Mom! Foxy lady! I swear you barely look 40 now. No one would ever suspect you're actually 50 and practically decrepit and senile."

Yes, Missouri admitted to herself, Jean Paul had done a fabulous job. But once she washed off the makeup and did her own hair, the same old, stodgy, fat woman would materialize in front of the mirror. She sighed regretfully and got out of her car.

Thelma answered the door immediately. "Goodness gracious, child, come on in here and give me a hug."

Missouri hugged her former teacher and stepped back. Mrs. Coley looked mostly like Missouri remembered. "Seeing you brings back wonderful high school memories for me. Art was my favorite class," she said, remembering how she dabbled with tempera, watercolor, clay, ink, graphite and charcoal. "And you were always encouraging me to be more creative."

Mrs. Coley shut the door behind Missouri. "You were one of the most talented students I ever had. When I heard you were getting married, I worried you might give up your art permanently. I'm happy you haven't."

Missouri smiled at her teacher and thought how good she looked. Her long brunette locks were mostly gray, but she still wore them up in a loose bun. The all-knowing bluish-gray eyes were now behind silver metallic-framed bifocals. Like herself, Thelma had picked up a few extra pounds and could be described as pleasantly plump, with chubby, dimpled cheeks and a very ample bosom. Her tiny heart-shaped mouth was no longer covered with fire engine red lipstick, but with a more subdued pale mauve.

"Mrs. Coley, it's so good to see you, again," blubbered Missouri as she gave her teacher another hug.

"Please, dear, you're old enough now to call me Thelma."

"Thelma. It may be difficult, but I'll give it a try."

Thelma ushered Missouri into a dark oak-paneled family room and seated her on a comfortable forest-green sofa with dark burgundy throw pillows. A painting of a field of sunflowers hanging over the gray stone fireplace mantle caught Missouri's attention as soon as she sat down. "That painting is beautiful," Missouri said as Thelma left the room, returning quickly with a tea tray.

"Thank you, dearie, that's one of Lamar Dodd's paintings that he did in Cortona before he died."

Missouri recognized the name of the well-known local artist who had been head of the art school for many years.

"Amazing how he continued to work even after heart surgery and his stroke." She poured Missouri a cup of tea and offered her a piece of homemade pound cake.

"Yes, I remember him. He did a lot of paintings of the heart after he had surgery." Missouri added sugar to her tea and stirred.

Thelma sat down on the sofa and poured herself a cup of tea. "And the other paintings and drawings in the room were done by students in Arthur's classes over the years."

"Arthur?" asked Missouri as she looked at the potpourri of artwork hanging on the walls. A large oil painting of a female nude dominated the far wall, banked by smaller nudes created in charcoal, pen and ink, conté crayon and pastels. The other walls held a variety of still lifes and landscapes.

"I'm sorry, dear. Yes, Arthur, my husband. He's a university art professor in the painting and drawing area, but he teaches one or two semesters each year in the Studies Abroad Program in Cortona."

Missouri dropped her cup noisily into her saucer. Her breathing quickened. "An art professor? I didn't even know you were married."

Thelma laughed heartily. "Of course not. High school students never want to believe their teachers have a life outside of the classroom."

"I'm sorry," apologized Missouri.

"Sorry I have a husband or sorry I'm married to Arthur?" Her eyes twinkled as she poured Missouri another cup of tea.

Flustered, Missouri took a deep breath. "Oh, no, that's not what I mean at all. I'm sorry that high school students are too caught up in their own lives to think about the lives of others."

"Sometimes, dearie, that can be a good thing. Now suppose you pass me that portfolio of yours. While you finish up the cake, I'll familiarize myself with your work."

Missouri sipped her tea and watched Thelma thumb through her artwork, stopping occasionally to pull out a piece for closer examination. From time to time she would make a comment out loud to herself such as "Oh, yes, I remember this one" or "Not bad" or "Good try." When finished, Thelma carefully replaced the artwork in the black portfolio. Then she looked at Missouri, her fingers thumping against the portfolio, deep in thought.

Missouri's heart sank. She knew she shouldn't have listened to Amelia and gotten her hopes up. She, Missouri Campbell Rothman, was just a fat, incompetent over-the-hill woman. "I'm sorry. I hope I didn't waste your time."

Thelma's head jerked straight up. "Waste my time? Why, child, that's preposterous. And stop apologizing. I am delighted to see you again, and I'm ecstatic to hear that you are interested in art school. You were one of my truly gifted students. Full of potential. I was terribly disappointed when you gave up college to marry the man of your dreams. But a woman often ends up following her heart and postponing her own desires."

"When I look back on my life," Missouri spoke softly, fighting back tears, "if I had to live it over, I would still marry Doyle. I was able to see the world, and we had two wonderful sons whom I love very much."

Thelma reached over and patted Missouri's hand. "There, there, dearie. I understand. You gave up college and your art, but it's not too late to fulfill your dreams."

Missouri wiped the corner of her right eye with her napkin and sniffed. "It's not? You really think there's a chance I could get into art school?"

"Yes, dearie, you can make it happen. While the university is processing your application, I want you to create some newer work for your portfolio. Do lots of portraits – that's where your strengths lie. Also, do a few watercolors, landscapes, a still-life or two – whatever you feel like doing. As soon as you get your acceptance letter, give me a call." Thelma stood up. "Now go home and get to work."

•   •   •   •   •

For several weeks, Missouri spent hours in front of a mirror doing self-portraits with graphite. On weekends, she sketched Cody sitting with his laptop.

Cody was impressed with his mother's work. "Mom, you're good. How come you never did this when we were growing up? You told us not to waste any of our God-given talents. You certainly hid this one really well. I think having an artist for a mother is totally cool."

Missouri stepped back from the portrait she had started of Michael using a photo of him in his Air Force uniform. "Thanks, Cody. I just hope I'm good enough to get into art school." She glanced critically at the drawing and attacked it with a kneaded eraser. "I think his nose is just a bit too wide."

Cody leaned over and watched her narrow the nose. "Yeah, that looks much better. Wow, Mom, that looks just like Michael. You should send that to him. He'll probably want to frame it."

"Maybe eventually, Cody, but now everything that looks halfway decent needs to go into my portfolio – in case I really do get accepted into the university."

"You'll get in, Mom. Maybe they'll give you a scholarship, too."

Missouri looked at her son and smiled. "I'm not holding my breath, but thanks for the thought, Cody. You're my number one cheerleader."

• • • • •

In early August, Missouri added three watercolor landscapes to the portfolio pile of artwork and stepped outside to get the mail. She ambled down the driveway to the mailbox. The door popped open with a clunk, exposing one magazine and one white #10 envelope bearing the University of Georgia logo. Her hand trembled when she pulled it from the mailbox.

As she walked the length of the driveway back to the house, she turned the envelope over and over in her hands, examining the bulk rate first-class metered postage and the return address from the admission's office at the university. Finally, she stuck a moist finger under a loose corner of the flap and tore an opening the full length of the envelope. She smiled to herself as she remembered how this annoyed Doyle, who meticulously opened each envelope with an ornate sterling silver letter opener. Sharp enough to do some real damage if stabbed into someone's back, she thought, pulling out the contents of the envelope. Holding her breath, she carefully unfolded the pages and straightened the bifocals on her nose.

"We are pleased..." The words were like brilliantly colored blinking neon lights. "Yes!" she screamed. "Holy dang it all!" She ran out the door screaming and did a victory dance on the front porch. "Hey, everybody! Hello, World! I'm going to college!"

Chapter Six

Thelma Coley was the first person Missouri called. As they chatted over the phone, Missouri pictured her former teacher with a big smile.

"Thank you so much for your help and support," Missouri said.

"I didn't do anything, dearie."

"I doubt if admissions would have accepted me without your glowing letter of recommendation."

"Don't sell yourself short, Missouri. You were accepted because of your high SAT score and your scholastic high school record. Now call your sons and tell them their mother is a college student. I know they'll be excited for you."

"I'm the one excited. Imagine **me** in college – at my age!"

Thelma laughed. "You're on a high at the moment. When you come back down to Earth, you will see that being a nontraditional student is difficult, but you can do it. Now comes the hard part – to get you into the art school. Bring all of your work over to the house tonight. We need to schedule you for a portfolio review as soon as possible."

Missouri did not respond.

"What's wrong?" asked Thelma. "You've been working, haven't you?"

"Every waking moment. I even put my job hunt on hold because I've been busy drawing and painting. It's just that..."

"What, dearie? What's the problem?"

Missouri could hear the concern in Thelma's voice. "Everything in my portfolio looks pathetic."

"Don't you worry, Missouri. Bring over your work and let me decide. You, my dear, don't give yourself and your artistic talent enough credit."

•   •   •   •   •

With masking tape, Thelma hung Missouri's artwork on the family room walls. She turned slowly around the room, studying each piece with a critical eye.

41

Methodically, she pulled down and set aside some of the work until only a dozen pieces remained on the walls. "All right, dearie, these works I consider your best ones. Do you agree with me?"

"Why do you think that one is so great?" Missouri pointed to one of her self-portraits.

"The eyes."

"My eyes?" she asked puzzled.

"Yes, dearie, you captured some very deep emotions in those eyes...anger...hurt...despair...fright...innocence lost...Can't you see it?"

"I'm not sure, but I certainly feel all of those emotions every day."

Thelma gave Missouri's hand a squeeze. "I promise you the pain will get better with time. You should take advantage of these intense feelings. Through your work, others can experience what you're feeling. That is good art."

Missouri reached over and hugged Thelma. "Thank you."

"You're welcome, dearie, but you're the one with the talent and you've worked very hard to show that you have it. You have an interview with the portfolio committee Tuesday at 2 p.m.

Missouri stepped back, her eyes brimming with tears. "I'm so scared. What if they hate my work?"

"You'll be fine. Your work is good. Trust me when I say you'll have one of the better portfolios."

• • • • •

As soon as Missouri heard she'd been accepted as a student in the Lamar Dodd School of Art, she immediately phoned Thelma and Amelia with the good news. Her third phone call went to Cody at the magazine office where he worked in Atlanta. "Woo hoo, you go, Mom! That's the best news I've heard today. Saturday night we'll celebrate at Five and Ten."

Missouri suddenly felt an icy, unsettling feeling in the pit of her stomach. Five and Ten, which served Southern food with French and Italian influences, was where Doyle always took her for special occasions like their anniversary, birthdays or Valentine's Day. "Cody, that's a nice thought, but could we celebrate somewhere else...maybe Sakura or the Last Resort?"

"What's wrong with Five and Ten, Mom? We always go there to...oh...right...sorry." Cody sighed. "I wasn't thinking. You choose the place and I'll pick up the tab."

By the time Missouri got around to calling Michael, it was about 10 o'clock in the morning in Misawa and he was at work. "Lt. Rothman here," he answered.

Michael sounded just like he was on the phone across the street. "Good morning, Michael."

"Mom!? Is everything all right?"

"Yes, Michael, everything is more than all right. I got my acceptance letter from the university. I start classes this fall."

"That's awesome, Mom. I'm glad you're doing this. What are you majoring in? Let me guess. Business? Or early childhood education so you can teach?"

"Neither, I'm enrolled in the College of Arts and Sciences."

"That's okay. A degree in political science or history will help you get a good job."

Missouri took a deep breath and exhaled slowly. "I'm majoring in art."

"Art?" A few seconds of silence passed. "Graphics design or scientific illustration or art education?"

"Actually, I've been accepted into the drawing and painting area. I want to be a portrait artist." Missouri cringed at the long period of silence. Just when she decided he'd hung up on her, he spoke up.

"Does Dad know about this?" asked Michael.

She could hear the chill in his voice. It was definitely time to end this conversation before it turned nasty. "My goodness. Just look at the time. This call is costing me a fortune, Michael. Tell Lizzie I said hello. Love you!" As Missouri hung up, she could hear Michael yelling her name. Oh bother, she thought. Michael will be calling his father right about now. Then she would get an earful from Doyle.

Sure enough, less than an hour later, the phone rang and it was Doyle. "Missouri?" His voice sounded shaky. Borderline angry with a forced calm. She held her breath. "I just talked to Michael."

"That's nice, Doyle. I'm glad you keep in touch with him."

"Don't patronize me, Missouri." His voice went up a decibel. "What's this about you going to the university this fall?"

"You heard correctly, Doyle. I'm finally getting my college education."

"Sitting around drawing pictures all day is not an education and I won't pay a dime for it, do you hear me?"

Doyle's anger and frustration did not surprise Missouri. She knew how he always had to be in control. How everything had to go his way. "I hear you

Doyle, but I talked to my lawyer. He says I can major in whatever pleases me, not you."

"Dammit, I don't care what your lawyer says."

Missouri was shaking all over. She could feel her heart beating faster. How she hated confrontation – especially with Doyle. She took a deep breath and hoped her voice wasn't quaking with fear. "Too bad, Doyle, because I care what he says. I'm majoring in art whether you like it or not." Missouri slammed down the receiver. A few seconds went by and the phone rang. Missouri picked it up. "Hello?"

"How dare you hang up on me!" yelled Doyle.

Missouri grinned and slammed down the receiver, again. She actually enjoyed the moment. A few seconds passed before the phone rang a third time. Missouri picked up the receiver half an inch and let it drop back in the cradle. Then she grabbed her sketch pad and pencils and went outside.

．　．　．　．　．

Missouri registered for four classes for fall semester: beginning drawing, beginning art history, English composition and math. As she fully expected, she was the oldest person in each of her classes. When she walked into math class – the last student to arrive before the professor – the class went silent, every eye was on her. As she stood at the door searching for an empty seat, a brunette on the front row raised her hand. "Are you teaching this class, because I signed up for Dr. Randolph's class."

Somewhat flustered, Missouri managed to smile down at the young woman and reply, "No, I'm a student just like you."

Dr. Randolph arrived as Missouri sat in the last empty seat. He did a quick roll call, pausing briefly when Missouri responded to her name. English class followed math, which was followed by a lunch break. Missouri found a bench under an oak tree and sat down. She took a turkey sandwich and a drink out of Cody's old high school backpack and relaxed.

After finishing her sandwich, Missouri took the Campus Express bus across campus to the Visual Arts Building. She did a quick exploration of all three floors of the building and the gallery spaces, and located her studio classroom. One entire back wall was glass windows, overlooking the creek and a shady green space. In the classroom, individual wooden benches were arranged in a circle around a small square platform. Missouri watched the other students straddle the benches like riding a horse and dropped her backpack to the floor. She noticed the other students had fishing tackle boxes full of art supplies and made a note to herself to buy one. Unable to believe that she was really enrolled in a college art class, she hugged herself and sighed happily.

"I haven't seen you before. This your first semester?" came a throaty voice behind her.

Missouri turned and saw not a young student, but a woman around her age with long, black curly hair, a low-neck peasant blouse that exposed lots of sagging cleavage, a long, flowery skirt, large silver loop earrings, a dozen or more silver bracelets, a bell-encrusted hip belt, and toe rings on her bare feet. Bohemian was the first thought that came to Missouri's mind.

"Yes," she spluttered. "I'm new." She stood and extended her hand. "Missouri Rothman."

"Nice to meet you, Missouri," the woman said, shaking her hand. "I'm Shirley Pendergrass, but most everyone calls me Magic."

"Magic?"

"Oh yeah, 'cause I can make you better like magic."

Missouri looked around the class room for help, but no one was looking her way. "I don't get it."

"Sit down on the bench and let me show you." Magic nudged Missouri to straddle the bench with her back to her. Then with her fingers on Missouri's shoulders, she began to slowly massage and knead her muscles.

Missouri instantly felt herself relaxing. A soothing, warm sensation oozed across her back and up her neck. "That feels so good," murmured Missouri, her eyes closed.

Shirley, a.k.a. Magic, dropped her hands and walked around to face Missouri, her bells jingling with each step. "And that's how I got my nickname." She plopped down on the bench across from Missouri and looked at her curiously. "I'm 55 years old, divorced twice, three grown children, four grandchildren and two chocolate Labs. How about you?"

Missouri was startled at her directness. "Uh...well, I'm 50 years old, newly divorced, two grown sons, no grandchildren and no pets."

"This is my second year at UGA. I'm in drawing and painting. What area are you hoping to be in?"

"I've been accepted into drawing and painting, too."

Magic tilted her head and eyed her warily. "Already? That's impossible. You aren't supposed to get a portfolio review until the end of your first semester.

45

How did you rate that?"

"I don't know," replied Missouri, dumbfounded. "I was told to bring my portfolio in for an interview and I did."

"Hmmmmm. I see," mumbled Magic, as she stood up. "Either you're very talented or you know important people in the right places."

Missouri's eyes widened. She didn't know how to respond to that, so she didn't.

"Yikes, I have to get to my figure drawing class. Nice meeting you, Missouri. See you around."

•   •   •   •   •

The first few weeks of beginning drawing seemed mundane, but Missouri worked hard -- first drawing straight lines, then progressing to sketching milk cartons, paper bags and draped material, and learning about shadows, depth of field and perspective. What she enjoyed best of all about her drawing class was her sketch book in which she sketched on a daily basis. After completing class assignments, she sat around campus, inside and out, drawing portraits on the sly.

What she liked least about art class was what happened towards the end of class, when everyone taped their work to the wall for a peer review. Ned Helm, her instructor and a graduate student, would point to a piece of work and ask for comments. Missouri hated every moment of it. She never wanted to say anything about anybody's work and she certainly didn't want anyone to criticize her own. During student comments, Ned would tug on his straggly carrot-red beard and nod. Then he would either agree or perhaps point out something no one else had noticed. But he rarely said anything about Missouri's work.

As the weeks went by, Missouri was starting to feel more confident about her work. The class experimented with different media. She loved drawing with graphite pencils. She especially loved the softer ones, like 6B, because she could smudge her lines. Charcoal pencils and *conté* crayons were okay, but charcoal sticks were too messy and fragile. She thought she would love pastels. They looked so bright and cheerful in the box, but she found if you blended and smudged too much, your drawing would become pure sludge on paper. Then there was ink and *gauche* -- so beautiful when Ned demonstrated how to use it, but pretty sucky when she tried.

The week before mid-terms, the class worked with clay. The first time

Missouri slammed a handful of clay down on the table to soften it up, she was instantly in love. The more she squeezed and shaped the clay, the more she felt the tension leaving her neck and shoulders. Ned instructed the class to take the clay home overnight and create something that would grab his attention.

Friday morning, Missouri lifted her creation out of a cardboard box and set it on the work table. She had taken one of the rocks that Doyle used to separate the grass area from the flower bed and made a rose – just like the ones she made in cake decorating class 20 years ago. After selecting the perfect rock, she hefted it in her hand and wondered if throwing it at Doyle would make her feel better. Probably not. After super-gluing her rose to the rock and adding a few leaves, she had taken out her acrylics and painted the rose black.

As a group, the class went from one table to another to discuss each clay creation. As usual, the students offered their comments first, then Ned added his. Missouri was impressed with what her classmates had created from clay – everything from a New Balance running shoe to a winged dragon. Missouri's table was the last stop. She wished she'd been first. Everyone was tired now and ready for class to be over. At first no one said anything. Then a tall, skinny student with a shaggy man-bun and goatee – Missouri thought his name was Ian – wiped his nose and cleared his throat. "You painted it?"

Missouri couldn't tell if he was asking because he wasn't sure she'd painted it or because he couldn't believe she'd painted it. She raised her chin. "Yes, I did."

"You painted it black?" he asked.

Was he blind? She spoke louder. "Yes, I did. I painted it black. I wanted it black. Okay?"

From behind the students surrounding Missouri's table, Ned walked around and stood between her and Ian. He spoke softly. "I believe that Ian is not criticizing you for painting the rose black. He just wants to know why you painted it black."

Missouri looked at Ned. What the crap did it matter that she'd painted the stupid rose black. Didn't he ask everyone to create something that would grab his attention? She took a deep breath, let it out slowly and looked directly at her instructor. "The black rose represents how I feel." Ned raised his eyebrow. "It represents the darkness and sadness in my heart."

Ned nodded. "If an artist can express his or her emotions through their art, then the finished art will reflect that emotion to everyone. Good job, Mrs. Rothman."

• • • • •

Right after mid-term, Ned Helm announced that once each week the class would have an opportunity to work with a nude model. "This work is of vital importance to your development as an artist. It must be taken seriously. There will be no giggling, no sniggering and no lewd or funny comments. All models must be treated with respect."

Missouri felt her stomach twitch. She had not expected to work with a nude model her first semester. She felt her face flush. She hoped the model would be a female because they were smooth and curvy. Males were lumpy. The model was male.

Ned introduced the model as Tony. The young man entered the studio barefoot and wearing a pink chenille bathrobe, several sizes too small. As he mounted the platform in the center of the studio, Missouri felt herself wanting to laugh. She bit her lip so hard, she tasted blood. The only naked male she'd ever seen, besides her sons when they were babies, was Doyle. And that was fine with her. How was she going to endure drawing a naked man without dying from embarrassment?

Tony the model was tall and thin with long gawky arms and legs and a concave, hairless chest. She could count every rib. Most of his eyes and pale face were hidden by his dirty blonde hair. While Ned adjusted the lights, Tony slipped off the robe and stood waiting, his shoulders slumped forward.

Missouri stared at Tony's flaccid penis hanging down between his thighs, slightly off-center to the left. Biting her lip, again, Missouri felt her cheeks begin to burn. She averted her eyes and carefully examined her charcoal pencil, making sure it didn't need sharpening. Finally Tony assumed a standing pose and Ned gave the class five minutes to capture an image.

Missouri concentrated on Tony's face and quickly drew a portrait before Ned called time. As the model assumed a new 15-minute pose, Ned strode over to Missouri and picked up her portrait. "Mrs. Rothman, we're paying this model by the hour so you can have an opportunity to sketch a nude figure," he said, returning her work. "Concentrate on the neck down. For this exercise today, the face is not important."

Missouri groaned and swallowed hard. What an idiot you are, she told herself, turning her attention to the whole Tony. Still, she avoided drawing the genitalia area, choosing instead to make it a dark, shaded blob.

Ned, who had been standing behind her as she finished drawing the figure, stepped forward and pointed to the large shaded spot where the thighs met the groin. "What is this dark area here, Mrs. Rothman?" he asked.

Missouri avoided his gaze and cleared her throat. "Uh...a shadow?"

Ned grunted and walked away. "I think you can do better," he said over his shoulder.

Missouri felt her cheeks burning. She covered her eyes. Missouri, you prude, she fussed at herself. It's only four inches of flesh-colored, wrinkled, circumcised penis. Get a grip. And by the end of class, she had covered a clean sheet of drawing paper with sketches of Tony's flaccid penis and hairless testicles.

●　　●　　●　　●　　●

The following week, Ned called for all sketch books to be turned in. Reluctantly and hesitantly, Missouri dropped off her book as she left class. She felt like she was leaving her first born on the steps of an orphanage. Several days later, Ned returned the sketch books. A note was attached to Missouri's asking her to remain after class to talk with him. Her stomach twisted. Could they boot you out of art school if your work wasn't any good? She remained on her bench at the end of class and watched the other students file out. Two students hovered with Ned for questions about the assignment, but soon left.

Ned looked over at Missouri and smiled encouragingly. "Let's go across the hall to my office."

Missouri followed him into his windowless corner office. Hundreds of art books were stuffed onto floor-to-ceiling shelves. A narrow path led from the doorway to his desk and two chairs. The rest of the floor space was taken up with wooden frames, some with painted canvases, but most of them empty. Tangles of hanging wire protruded into the cleared path like brambles that had to be sidestepped. Ned sat down in the chair behind his desk and indicated the other for her.

"Thank you for staying after class, Mrs. Rothman," he began. "I was very impressed with the drawings in your sketch book."

Missouri felt a rush of heat and color to her cheeks. She looked down at her art box. "Thank you."

"I liked your portraits and caricatures best. I think you have lots of talent in that area." Missouri's head bobbed up and she looked directly into his eyes. "I hope you won't mind, but I showed your work to another faculty member in the drawing and painting area, Ronald Sherman. Do you know him?"

Missouri shook her head. "No, I don't know anyone in the art school except you."

Ned smiled. "Then it's time you met Ron. He's a member of the Atlanta Portrait Society."

Missouri sucked in a quick breath. "He paints portraits?"

"Yes, he paints portraits. In fact, he is quite well known for his portraits. He receives commissions from all over the world."

Missouri felt her heartbeat quicken. She couldn't believe there was a university faculty member here who specialized in painting portraits. "That's wonderful. I'd love to see some of his work," she said, moving to the edge of her seat.

"That's good, because he's very interested in meeting you." Ned took a pencil and wrote down a phone number and address for Ron's studio. "He will be at his studio today until 5 o'clock."

Excited and nervous, Missouri tripped over something as she was leaving Ned's office, but she managed not to fall on her face. Stupid old woman, she screamed to herself as she tried to gracefully regain her balance.

Ned reached out a hand to help steady her. "Are you okay? Sorry this studio is such a landmine. I share this space with two other graduate teaching assistants. "

"No problem. It's my fault. I wasn't looking where I was going." She could feel the heat in her cheeks. She turned to flee his office. "Thanks, Mr. Helm. I appreciate your interest." She waved to him over her shoulder.

Ned waved back. "Let me know how it goes. See you in class Wednesday."

• • • • •

Ron Sherman's spacious studio was located in a large gray metal building with a red tin roof. Three other artist studios were housed in the same building. All occupied by art professors – not graduate student instructors. The entrance to Ron's studio was through two heavy-duty, double metal doors with a small glass window in each. The windows were papered over for privacy. Ron's name and studio hours were typed on an index card in one corner. After knocking as loud as she could on the metal door, she heard a man's voice yell out, "Door's open, come in."

Ron sat in front of an easel with natural light pouring in from an overhead skylight. He had long white hair fastened at the nape of his neck, bushy white eyebrows, and a white beard and mustache. That along with a big smile, rosy cheeks and pale blue eyes made Missouri think of Santa Claus on vacation. She guessed him to be in his mid-60s.

Picking up a rag, Ron wiped off his hands and stood up. "You must be Missouri Rothman," he spoke with a melodious voice. "Ron Sherman."

Missouri reached out her hand and Ron shook it firmly, holding it a trifle second longer than she was used to. "Nice to meet you, Mr. Sherman," she replied, freeing her hand from his.

"Please, call me Ron. May I call you Missouri?" She nodded. "I'm glad you could stop by my studio so we can talk about your work. Your portrait drawings are very good. I recognized many of the students and faculty members that you drew. You did an excellent job capturing their facial expressions and unique personalities with your pencil and pen."

Missouri's eyes roamed the studio. She was resisting the urge to browse through the many canvases propped up around his studio. "Thank you. I really love faces. I study people's faces to see what features make each person unique."

"Yes, I can see in your work that you love what you're doing. I can feel your passion. That's why I'd like for you to consider taking an independent study with me next semester."

Missouri drew her hand to her throat. "Me? You want to teach me?" Her soprano voice almost squeaked.

He chuckled. "Yes, I want to work with you. But before you agree to an independent study with me, you should know that I am quite demanding and very critical. Any of my students will tell you this. I will work you into the ground and then insist you get up and try harder. But by the end of the semester, if you can stick it out, all of the techniques you learn from me will make you a better portrait artist. Knowing this, are you willing to make the commitment?"

Missouri furrowed her brows in confusion. "Let me make sure I understand this. You would like to work with me one on one next semester?"

He frowned. "Do you have a problem with that?"

"I...uh...I mean...it's just that...well..."

Ron raised his brows and crossed his arms. "Take your time, Missouri. I don't want you to rush into anything you're not ready for. But I do have a class to teach in about 15 minutes."

"I'm sorry...it's just that you caught me by surprise." She looked him in the eye. "This is my first semester of art school. I feel inadequate."

"Yes, I see that," he said and almost seemed to be on the verge of a smile. "But you're also extremely talented, even if you haven't realized it yet." Ron busied himself washing and drying his hands. "All I need from you is a simple yes or no. If you say no, I have a dozen students who are begging to take that space."

"Yes!" she blurted out. "I would like that more than anything."

"Good. I'll make the arrangements." He pointed the way to the door. "Thank you for stopping by, Missouri. I'm looking forward to working with you next semester."

As Missouri left his studio, his words echoed in her mind. She gave herself a hug. Yes, Missouri, you are an extremely talented woman – for an old, fat, stupid lady.

. . . . .

On Tuesdays and Thursdays, Missouri had only the one class in art history. On these days and the weekend, she went to the YWCO. With the help of her personal trainer and nutritionist, she began losing a few pounds. She also noticed some positive changes in her body shape. By Thanksgiving break, she had lost 15 pounds and one dress size. Ecstatic, she took several boxes of the large-size clothes to the Episcopal Thrift House. She figured if she didn't have any fat clothes to squeeze back into, she wouldn't gain her weight back. From the back of her closet she pulled out pants and skirts she'd put away years ago when they became too tight to button. And now they fit perfectly.

During the Christmas holidays, Missouri took her new portfolio of work over to Thelma Coley's house. "My dear, these are very good," said Thelma, as she studied each piece. "I especially like this still life with the baby doll and roses."

"Thanks. Ned liked it, too. He chose it and one of my student portraits to display in the fall exhibition of student drawings."

"Sorry I didn't get to campus to see that during the few days it was up," Mrs. Coley said.

Missouri grinned and took out her cell phone. "I took several photos of my two pieces hanging on the gallery wall." She found the photos and passed the phone to her former teacher. "When Cody saw the exhibit, he insisted on taking a photo of me standing next to my work."

"Ned chose well." Mrs. Coley smiled and returned the phone to Missouri. "I may have missed the exhibition, but Arthur saw it and told me about it. Now, dearie, tell me about Ron Sherman. Arthur says you're going to be doing an independent study with him next semester. What an honor and quite out of the ordinary for him to accept a first-year student like yourself. He must have seen talent and potential in your work."

"I was absolutely speechless when he told me. I'm sure he thought I was some mindless twit. I hope I won't disappoint him."

"Nonsense. It's to his advantage that his *protégées* do their best work. I know you'll do just that."

• • • • •

True to his word, Ron Sherman worked Missouri relentlessly. From the first week of spring semester classes, she found herself devoting more time to her independent study than to the rest of her classes total. Even though she had no time for family and friends or a life outside of art school, she made time for her stress-relieving trips to the YWCO. The semester passed in a flash.

At a midterm work session, Ron told Missouri he had a surprise for her and could she meet him downtown at Starbuck's at 4 p.m. Although startled at his request, Missouri agreed. He was already waiting for her when she arrived and treated her to a cup of coffee just the way she liked it – a cup of hot milk with a spoonful of coffee for flavor.

"Did you know there is an art gallery on College Square?" he asked, watching her pour sugar into her mug.

"The one upstairs over the bar?" She took a sip of her hot milky coffee and waited.

"Yes, that's right. Throughout the year the owners exhibit work by local artists."

"I went up there once to see an exhibit of teapots and teacups. Why? What about it?" She thought perhaps Ron was having a one-man show and wanted her to see it.

Grinning, he reached over and grasped her hands in his. "I've made arrangements for you to have a one-woman show in three weeks."

Missouri felt her face flush with excitement. "What? You're not teasing me, are you?"

Ron squeezed her hands tightly and released them. He chuckled. "No, Missouri, I don't tease about things this serious." He stood up. "Come on, let's take a look at the space and I'll introduce you to the gallery owner."

. . . . .

Missouri stood at the top of the stairs and looked at the huge room. "I don't know, Ron. I couldn't possibly have enough good pieces to fill up this space."

Ron grabbed her shoulder and turned her around to face him. He tilted her chin up. "Look at me, Missouri. Not only do you have enough work to fill this room, your portraits are exceptional."

Missouri felt a tingle in her stomach. Could it be true...could she really be talented? "You're sure?" she asked softly.

He put his arms around her and gave her a hug. "Yes, I'm sure. This weekend we'll get together, go through your portraits and pick out your best ones. Then we'll get them all framed and ready to hang."

Her head spinning from the news, Missouri couldn't wait to get home and call Cody and Thelma.

. . . . .

By the day of the opening reception, Missouri was so nervous her stomach felt nauseous. She sat on her bed in tears. Cody, who came home for the weekend and the opening reception, heard his mother's sobs and went to see what was wrong. He sat on the bed beside her, gave her a hug and kissed her forehead. "Mom, today is your special day. You should be smiling and laughing. What's wrong?"

Missouri hugged Cody back tightly. "I don't think I can do this, Cody. You go and give my apologies."

Cody sighed. "This is just a case of stage fright. You'll be okay."

Missouri pulled herself away from Cody and wiped her eyes on his proffered handkerchief. "What if everybody hates my work? What if nobody comes?"

"Will you listen to yourself! Where's all that newly found self-confidence that got you this far? Where have all these doubts come from? You're being unfair to yourself. First of all, you know that everyone is not going to love your work. You yourself never liked Dalí or Picasso, right? As for nobody coming...I'll be there. Thelma Coley will be there. And your professors. Does it really matter to you if no one else comes?"

Missouri smiled at her son. "Thank you, Cody. You're right. I'm being silly and having a case of opening jitters."

Cody stood up. "Good, now shake a leg and get dressed."

Missouri still sat on the bed, a strickened look on her face. "Oh, no! I have nothing to wear."

•   •   •   •   •

Attired in svelte black velvet pants and jacket over a low-cut lacy red camisole, Missouri felt bolstered by Cody's wolf whistle as she'd exited the bedroom to leave for the gallery.

"Mom, you look gorgeous! Everyone will look at you, instead of your portraits." Missouri had Cody to thank for what she was wearing. He had found the outfit in the back of her closet in a garment back. Never worn, it had been purchased many years ago in a smaller size to encourage weight loss. Something that had not happened until now.

With long gold and black earrings nearly brushing her shoulders and her short curly auburn bob glistening in the gallery lighting, she made her entrance.

Ron spotted her across the room and met her halfway, clasping her hand and bussing her cheeks. "Why Mrs. Rothman, you clean up nicely," he said.

Quickly covering her embarrassment, Missouri introduced him to Cody.

Ron shook Cody's hand. "Good to meet you, Cody. I hope you realize you have a very talented mother."

"Yes, sir! I've always known she was extra special," he said, smiling at his mother.

Ron gently nudged Missouri to turn and quickly pointed out a reporter from the local daily newspaper, as well as a curator from an Atlanta gallery. "Also, if you look next to the charcoal drawing you did of Ned..." Missouri turned her head and saw a tall, slender, bespectacled middle-age man. "That's Terry Bruner, dean of arts and sciences."

"I've always wondered what he looked like," she said, as Ron wandered off in the dean's direction. Should she have gone with him, she wondered? She didn't do well meeting strangers, so she stayed where she was, watching Cody walk through the exhibit.

"I see that I was right about you."

Missouri turned around to find Magic coming up behind her. She noticed that today Magic was not barefooted. She had on a pair of flip-flops. "Hello, Magic. I'm glad you could come see my work. What do you mean, you were right about me?"

"Remember that first day I saw you? I said you either knew someone in high places or you were talented. I see I was right on both counts." Magic nodded her head toward Ron, who was busy talking to the dean.

Missouri fidgeted uncomfortably. Once again she wasn't sure how to respond to Magic. "I don't know what you mean. Mr. Sherman is just my professor."

"Yes, but Mr. Sherman is very picky about whom he accepts for an independent study."

"Yes, I've heard that from several people, too. I feel privileged that he accepted me."

"Just don't let it go to your head," replied Magic, as she turned and headed off toward the punch bowl. "Tootle loo," she said, tossing her hand in a wave of dismissal.

Shaking her head in wonder, Missouri began to circle the gallery space, looking for familiar faces, then freezing in her tracks when she saw Doyle standing in front of a pastel portrait of Cody. She was pretty sure she felt her heart thud to the floor. Her chest tightened and she suddenly found it difficult to breathe.

Before she could find an escape route, Doyle turned and spotted her. He raised his eyebrows, his eyes widened in surprise, and his jaw dropped. Seemingly in slow motion, he began walking towards her with a puzzled expression on his face. "Missouri?" he asked, as if in doubt of her identity.

Resigned to speaking to her ex-husband, Missouri forced herself to smile and step forward to greet him as if he were someone she truly wished to see. Reluctantly, yet politely, she extended her hand to Doyle. "Good evening, Doyle. How nice of you to come to my exhibition. I didn't know you knew about my show." Or even cared, she thought.

Doyle literally gaped at Missouri, his mouth opened and closed in silence. As though in shock from seeing his made-over ex-wife. Not taking his eyes off of her, Doyle opened his mouth, again, and finally words came out. "Wow! You look good." He swallowed hard. "Really good." He took a deep breath. "You've lost a lot of weight."

"Oh, maybe a few pounds." Missouri was amused and surprised at Doyle's astonishment. As long as he continued to be polite, she thought she could stand to be in the same room with him.

"I like your hair cut short like that, too. And you look quite stunning in that outfit."

Missouri did not know what to think about Doyle's compliments. She thought he sounded sincere enough, but she couldn't remember so many nice things coming out of his mouth at once. At least not since their honeymoon. "Thank you."

Doyle didn't say anything more. He just continued to stare at her with this funny goofy expression on his face. Missouri glanced around the gallery. "If you're looking for Cody," she pointed, "he's over there between the pimento cheese sandwiches and the fruit plate. Now, if you'll excuse me, I need to speak to some of the other guests." As she turned away from Doyle, she glimpsed an emotion flicker briefly across his face. Wistfulness or maybe regret, she wondered? Then she shook her head, fussed at herself and headed across the room to Thelma Coley.

Arm-in-arm, Missouri and her former art teacher walked around the gallery space to view each piece of artwork. They paused in front of a *conté* crayon portrait of a brooding young man, nude from the waist up. "Sam Huckabee," Missouri said. "A model in my anatomy and figure drawing class. I decided to focus on his face, rather than the full figure."

"Missouri, dear, this is the best piece in the entire show."

"You think so?" Missouri stepped back and looked at the work, trying to see what made it so great.

"Yes, I agree with you, Thelma," said a voice behind them.

Thelma turned and put her hand through the arm of an older man. "Why Arthur, how good of you to come."

Arthur reached out and shook Missouri's hand. "Hello, Missouri. We haven't been properly introduced. I'm Arthur Coley. I've heard so much about you and your work, I feel like I already know you."

"Same here," replied Missouri. As she did with each new face, she noted Arthur's full head of salt-and-pepper hair, dimples, round rosy cheeks and a heart-shaped mouth. Just like Thelma's. They were even the same height and carried the same girth around the middle.

"Yes," agreed Arthur, studying the portrait of the male model, "you did an excellent job with Sam. I know him personally and you've captured his essence 100 percent. It's all right there in his eyes and the jut of his chin."

"You are so right about that, Arthur," said Ron, walking up behind him. "Look really close. Those eyes are saying, 'If I don't finish my outside drawings for old Coley's class, I won't be graduating in June.'"

When the laughter died down, Ron turned to Missouri. "I think I speak for the entire drawing and painting area when I say you've done an outstanding job. Arthur, Ned and I think you should spend the next two years at the Old Masters Academy of Art."

"Florence? In Italy?" Missouri couldn't believe what she'd heard. She figured that Ron was being funny, again.

"*Si, Florenza*," replied Ron with an Italian accent.

"Arthur teaches at the university's Study Abroad Program in Cortona," pointed out Thelma.

"Italy is a great place to learn the classical method of drawing and painting," Arthur added enthusiastically.

Missouri looked at the Coleys and Ron as though they had just arrived on Earth from Mars. She backed away from what she saw as a trio of raving lunatics. "You want me to pack up and go by myself to live in a foreign country for two years?" she asked in disbelief.

Thelma raised a hand toward Arthur and Ron to silence them. "Why don't you two have a cup of punch and let me talk with Missouri." Thelma waited until the men were out of hearing distance, then she put her arm around Missouri's waist and guided her toward two chairs in a quiet corner of the gallery. "There, there, dearie," she tutted sympathetically and patted Missouri's hand. "You'll have to overlook Arthur and Ron. They were caught up in the moment and ambushed you. My goodness, dearie, you're shaking all over. Are you okay?"

"I'm sorry, Thelma, it's just that...well, you know..." How could she explain to her former teacher that life was pushing her along too fast? That she wanted to put on the brakes and drive at a more leisurely pace. Enjoy the scenery along the way.

Thelma looked at Missouri sympathetically. "Yes, I understand perfectly, dearie. You've come a long, long way since your divorce. It took a lot of courage for you to start college at your age." Thelma squeezed her shoulder. "But life is short and you have talent and abilities that other students don't have. You're quite gifted. Studying in Italy will be very beneficial for you. It's not like you've never been out of the country. Didn't you live in Naples for three years?"

Missouri nodded. "Yes, but I was there with my family."

"Did you enjoy living in Italy?"

"Of course I did. I loved everything about it."

"And didn't you do some watercolors while you were there?"

Missouri sighed. "Yes, but..."

"And you learned Italian, right?"

Missouri eyed her friend speculatively. "Some, but I've probably forgotten what I learned. Why, what's your point?"

Thelma clasped Missouri's hands in her own. "You have many happy memories of the years you spent in Italy. While you were there, you learned coping skills for living in a foreign country."

Missouri sat silently and thought about what Thelma had said. Yes, she had loved Italy. She and Doyle had been able to travel to areas outside of Naples, like Rome, Sorrento, the Isle of Capri and Pompeii. They had wanted to visit Florence and Venice, but were never able to travel that far away after Cody was born. But would she be able to return to Italy by herself? "I would love to see Michelangelo's 'David' and visit the Uffizi."

"Of course you would," Thelma said eagerly. "And the Pitti Palace, the Duomo, the Bargello, Santa Croce, Piazza della Signoria, Palazzo Vecchio, Ponte Vecchio, Italian pasta, gelato, biscotti, chianti..."

Missouri covered her ears and laughed. "Okay, okay, okay. Please, that's enough."

"In addition, you would be able to see in person all the famous works by the Old Masters while studying. What an opportunity."

"The benefits of studying abroad do not fall on deaf ears. I'm not stupid!" Missouri gasped at her words.

Thelma smiled. "I'm glad you finally realize that."

Missouri smiled back. Yes, she thought, I am not as stupid as I thought. I am not quite as fat as I used to be. But I'm still old and getting older.

Chapter Seven

During the last weeks of spring semester, Missouri thought a lot about studying in Florence. She talked with Ron, Arthur and Thelma, and by phone with Amelia. While she was trying to make a decision, she mailed in her Study Abroad application, accompanied by "glowing" letters of recommendation from Ron, Ned and Thelma. The important thing, Ron pointed out, was to apply before the deadline for fall semester. If she were accepted into the program, she could still elect not to go.

Her acceptance letter to the Old Masters Academy of Art arrived the last day of spring semester. Like her acceptance letter to the university the previous year, this one buoyed her spirits. Even though Missouri was elated to be selected for the program, she was anxious at the thought of actually participating.

When Cody heard about the acceptance letter, he didn't seem as enthused as he had when she first applied. Missouri didn't understand why. For dinner that night, he prepared one of his favorite dishes, *bean tostitos* with lettuce, tomatoes, guacamole, sour cream, chopped olives, cheddar cheese and salsa. But whereas he usually ate three or four to her one, tonight he barely made it through two. He just wasn't his cheerful, talkative self.

After cleaning the kitchen, Cody sat on the sofa next to Missouri. He responded to Missouri's questions with as few words as possible and never looked her in the eye. Finally she couldn't stand it any longer. "Okay, Cody, spit it out! What's wrong?"

He eyed her warily. "What makes you think something's wrong?"

Missouri shook her head. She leaned over and kissed his cheek. "You're brooding. That has always been the signal that something's bothering you. What's up? Trouble at work? That new girlfriend? What?"

Cody sighed and squirmed in his seat. "Ahhh, Mom. It's this Italy thing, I guess."

"What about it?" She couldn't understand how that was his problem.

He finally looked at her. Today he wore a blue shirt that turned his hazel eyes blue. "Are you serious about going?"

She breathed in deeply and let it out slowly. "I haven't made a decision either way. I'm still weighing the pros and cons. Why?"

"I'm glad you haven't decided for sure," he said, sounding relieved. "When do you have to let them know?"

"Next week. Classes start in August, but I would need to go a few weeks earlier for orientation."

"Does Dad know about this?"

"Not unless you told him. Or Michael." Because Missouri knew that if it went in Michael's ear, it would go from Michael's mouth to Doyle's ear. "What business is it to your dad if I study abroad?"

Cody shrugged. "I haven't said a word to either of them, but you know Dad will not be happy once he finds out."

"If I decide to go, your dad will know once my lawyer starts talking to him about tuition and other expenses. Then Michael will hear it from him, unless you tell your brother first."

Cody rubbed the back of his neck. "Before you make any decisions, I think you should know something."

"What?" Missouri held her breath, wondering what Cody could possibly say that might affect her decision? Was Doyle marrying Pamelynn or had he come down with something terminal?

He glanced down at his fidgety fingers and cleared his throat. "Erhmm...uh..." He swallowed hard. "Dad and Pamelynn broke up." He pulled nervously on his earring.

Missouri gasped and looked away. That was the last thing she had expected to hear. If Cody had said Doyle lost his job at the university or that his apartment had burned down, she could have dealt with that. But not this. She stood up and strode over to the glass sliding door and looked out across the backyard. "When did this happen?"

"This weekend," he answered, following her to the sliding door. "But Dad's been miserable ever since your gallery exhibit."

She turned to face him. "And you're telling me this now because...?"

"I thought you should know before you make a decision about going to Italy."

"I don't understand, Cody."

"I thought you might want to stay in town, in case there was a chance you and Dad could work things out and get back together."

Missouri could feel herself bristling. "Maybe your father doesn't want to work things out."

"Oh, but he does, Mom. Every time we talk, he goes on and on about seeing you at the gallery reception and how good you look now. I think he regrets all the pain he put you through."

"Is that exactly what he said, that I look good now?"

Cody nodded. "You do, Mom. You look absolutely fantastic. You're a new woman, Dad says so."

Seething inside, Missouri opened the door and walked outside. Everything was green and beautiful. The birds were singing and sharing the bird feeder. The squirrels were fussing at the birds. It was a great day to be alive. But she felt cold and numb. "Tell me, Cody. Has your father said one word to you about my artwork?"

"Uh...I don't remember."

"Strange that you don't remember something as important as that."

"Mom, I'm just not sure."

"You aren't sure Cody, because he never mentioned my artwork, did he?" Missouri whirled around, glaring at her son. "He only noticed that his old, fat, stupid wife had lost weight, shaped up and was looking good. Am I wrong?"

Cody looked away from Missouri and appeared agitated. "Why does that matter? Seems that the important thing is that Dad has dumped Pamelynn and wants to reconcile with you." He wiped his eyes with the back of his hand. "Is it wrong of me to hope that my parents can make up and get back together?"

Missouri quickly embraced her son. "I'm so sorry, Cody. I understand what's going on here." She kissed his cheek. "Thanks for letting me know about your dad." Yes, she thought, she would definitely take that valuable piece of information and stick it on her list of reasons to go to Florence.

· · · · ·

Ron was elated that Missouri had decided to go to Florence. "Happy day!" He embraced her. "To celebrate, I'm taking you out to dinner tonight."

"Thanks, I'd like that."

"Excellent. Meet me in the lobby of the Georgia Center at 6:30 p.m. and we'll dine in the Savannah Room."

· · · · ·

Missouri arrived a few minutes before the appointed time and sat down to wait for Ron. The Georgia Center for Continuing Education was a conference center on campus, which had two dining facilities open to the public, one cafeteria-style and one sit-down with tablecloths and cloth napkins – the Savannah Room.

Ron arrived right on time with a gift-wrapped package, which he handed to her. "With my best wishes for great artistic success."

Her cheeks blushing, she thanked him and they headed into the restaurant. Missouri ordered her favorite entree, the Celestial Chicken served over rice. The Southern-fried strips of chicken breast were not on her new healthy eating diet, but it always tasted delicious and tonight she was celebrating. Obviously, one could not count fat grams and carbs and celebrate at the same time. Ron must have been going for flavor over fat, too, since he requested the same.

"Thank you for suggesting this, Ron. I love to eat here, but I haven't been here in a long time...not since..." Her voice trailed off without completing the sentence.

"Not since you were here with your ex?" he asked sympathetically.

"Please, let's not ruin our dinner by mentioning that man." She forced a smile.

He leaned forward across the table, speaking softly. "Before we proceed to a happier dinner conversation topic, I just want to say that Doyle Rothman was a fool to let you go."

Missouri's eyes stung as she fought back the tears. "Thank you." She dabbed her eyes with her napkin. "Okay, next topic."

Ron smiled encouragingly. "How about Florence and you can open your present now."

Missouri's mouth formed an O. She reached under her napkin and brought out Ron's gift. Carefully she untied the ribbon and took off the wrapping paper. Inside was a classic-bound sketchbook covered with a hand-carved leather jacket. A narrow leather tie wrapped around a leather button to keep the book closed when not in use. "It's beautiful," she said, running her fingers over the pattern on the cover. "Did you make this yourself?"

"Hardly. Leatherwork doesn't fall under my area of expertise. One of my students, who is doing an apprenticeship at a leather company, creates and sells these. He says the English majors buy them for writing journals. I bought it for you as a combination sketchbook and journal for your adventures in Italy." He reached over and pointed at the cover. "That's a Celtic design to ward off evil spirits and brings the user good luck."

Missouri opened the book and examined the empty white pages. "Then I definitely need this. Thank you!"

Ron leaned forward. "Are you excited? Nervous? Apprehensive? Scared?"

"All of the above, but I have so much to do to get ready that I don't have time to think about it."

"That's good. Did your passport arrive?"

"Yes, yesterday."

"Have you been practicing your Italian?"

"I didn't learn that much when Doyle and I lived in Naples, so I'm taking a class in beginner's conversational Italian."

"*Molto bene!*"

"That's easy for you to say."

A waitress poured Ron a cup of coffee. "Missouri, you are going to experience and learn more than you would ever think possible." Ron stroked his beard. "I spent two years studying art in Florence about 40 years ago. It was the best two years of my life. I'm sure it will be that way for you, too. Your life will never be the same once you return. Your studies abroad will shape you and your art forever."

As Missouri listened to Ron, she broke out in goose bumps and the hair on her arms and the back of her head stood up. His excitement and enthusiasm were contagious. "Shall I send you a postcard?"

"Absolutely," he replied without hesitation. "I want to hear about everything, but don't spend too much time writing cards and letters or you won't have time to learn about Italian art or create your own masterpieces or enjoy your stay in Florence." He reached out and clasped her hands in his. "Missouri, you aren't going to believe how this will affect you. I'll write to you and when you get back, I want to hear all about your experiences."

Missouri nodded. She hoped that the trip would really become a reality. If she sat still and allowed her mind to wander, the doubts would begin. This would be her first real trip alone. She had only herself to depend on. No matter how thin, attractive and intelligent she appeared on the outside, on the inside she was feeling insecure and scared.

. . . . .

Her new passport lay on the coffee table beckoning her to Tuscany. She gripped the phone receiver tighter as Doyle's voice droned on. "Have you heard anything I've said, Missouri?"

Missouri opened up the passport and ran her finger over the photo. "Yes," she whispered. "I heard every word." She thought her voice sounded meek, subservient and distant.

"After seeing you at the gallery, I haven't been able to get you out of my mind. I've been a real idiot. I want us to make another go at it. Let me take you out for dinner tonight. We can talk about us and getting back together. I should have listened to you when our marriage went wrong. We just need some marriage counseling. What do you say?"

A tear slowly rolled down Missouri's cheek. She remembered last year – it seemed like another lifetime – how she'd begged Doyle to go to counseling with her. How she'd pleaded with him not to throw away 32 years of marriage. Even after the divorce was final, she'd still hoped he would have second thoughts. And now, after she was putting her broken life back together – making lemonade out of her lemons – now that she'd accepted the divorce and moved on – now that he was tired of his nubile little sex pot – now, **he** was the one who wanted to put the pieces of their marriage back together. But was she willing to give up her dreams, again, for a chance to have him back in her life?

Everything was in place for her trip to Italy. The house-sitter, a graduate student of Arthur Coley's, was ready to move in. And since Missouri was determined to go, Cody agreed to come home every other weekend to sort through the mail and pay the bills. She felt like she was at the starting gate waiting for the gun to go off.

Doyle's voice continued in her ear, oblivious to no response coming from her end. "The boys and I think this whole study abroad thing is ridiculous, Missouri. You're too old to go traipsing off to Italy for two years. You're not twenty-something any more. Besides, Italy is a Third World country — a dangerous place to be. Where do you think the Mafia came from? The country is a hotbed for terrorists and communists. Stay here with me. We'll go to counseling, get back together and I'll let you take all the art classes you want. What do you say?"

"Doyle..." she began and stopped. What did he mean by "all the art classes you want"? Missouri swallowed hard and tried to find her voice.

"Missouri..." Doyle crooned out her name. "If you ever loved me and our sons, you'll stay here and help me rebuild our marriage."

A knot twisted in Missouri's stomach and her teeth clenched tightly. "Doyle, if you ever cared for me, you'll understand why I have to do this." She quietly hung up the phone.

Chapter Eight

As the plane made its approach to the Florence airport, Missouri looked down on rolling hills and farmland, which gave way to beige and ochre-colored buildings topped with orange-red roofs. During the plane's final descent, she saw long, slender cypress trees and olive groves. Then the wheels touched down on the tarmac. She had arrived. It was the first day of the rest of her life.

With a full backpack straining her shoulders and pulling a maximum-capacity-packed 36-inch Pullman suitcase, Missouri exited customs in Florence. Directly in front of her, she saw a young woman holding an Academy of Art sign and a clipboard. She wheeled her suitcase in that direction.

The woman smiled as Missouri approached. "*Buongiorno*," she greeted Missouri. "Are you American?"

"*Si, mi chiamo* Missouri Rothman. *Sono di Georgia*," she said, introducing herself. "*E Lei?*"

"*Piacere, Missouri. Mi chiamo Alessandra DeMarco.* I am the foreign student coordinator for the Old Masters Academy of Art," she said in heavily accented English and shook Missouri's hand. "You speak some Italian already, yes?"

"*Si, un piccolo*," Missouri answered, pinching her thumb and index finger nearly together.

Alessandra laughed. "You'll be fluent in no time."

After checking Missouri's name off her list, Alessandra led her to a weary group of students standing or sitting on either suitcases or the floor. "*Attenzione*, everyone. This is Missouri Rothman from Athens, Georgia, in America. She is the last one." Everyone cheered so loudly, Missouri couldn't help but wonder how long they'd been waiting for her arrival. Quickly the students grabbed their belongings and followed Alessandra to ground transportation and a waiting bus.

•   •   •   •   •

The Academy of Art, a small urban visual arts college, was quite different from a major research university with a large sprawling campus. The Academy was located near the famous Palazzo Pitti, built in the 1400s by wealthy banker Luca Pitti, who went bankrupt trying to outrival the Medici family through a display of wealth and power.

Missouri soon learned that the Palazzo Pitti and the Academy were located in an area of Florence across the River Arno known as the Oltrarno. The main thoroughfare, Via Maggio, was always bustling, especially the end closer to the river and the tourists. But the side streets were home to small residences, quiet squares, arty shops, studios, workshops and reasonably priced restaurants. A good neighborhood for artists and students.

Missouri was assigned to a one-bedroom student apartment on the third floor of a 13th-century restored *palazzo* only a few blocks from the school. The building was older than dirt. No elevator on the premises, Missouri had to lug her suitcase slowly and tediously up several flights of well-worn stone steps. She was astonished that halfway up one flight of stairs, a second set of stairs would often branch off and lead up to an apartment door. Hers was one of these.

Thanking herself for enduring all those weeks of lifting weights and running on the Y's treadmill, she arrived huffing and puffing at the wide metal door to her apartment. Carefully, she inserted a large medieval-looking key into the lock. The locking mechanism clicked loudly and the door moved slowly inward, creaking noisily as it opened. A long-haired brunette reclining on a sofa inside the front room startled and dropped the book she was reading onto the terra cotta floor. "Sorry," apologized Missouri, pulling and tugging on her suitcase as she tried to get it through the door. "Didn't mean to frighten you."

The woman hurriedly arose from the sofa to offer assistance with the heavy problem. "You didn't frighten me," she said with a French accent. "The art history book put me to sleep and the noise of the opening door jolted me awake."

Taking a closer look, Missouri saw that the woman was not as young as she first thought. Maybe mid-forties, she decided, but it was hard to tell.

Her suitcase safely inside and the front door closed and bolted, Missouri and the woman collapsed on the sofa. "How did you manage to get that heavy suitcase up the stairs?" the woman asked.

"One step at a time," Missouri answered, still breathing hard from her efforts.

The woman laughed and held out her hand. "Welcome to Florence. I am

Gabriella Du Fiore from Nice, France. You are from America, *oui?*"

"*Oui*...uh...yes. Actually, I'm from Athens, Georgia, in the southeastern part of the United States. She shook Gabriella's hand. "My name is Missouri Rothman."

"Missouri? Like the big American river and the state of Missouri?"

She smiled. "Yes, that Missouri."

"A most unusual name for an American woman, *n'est-ce pas?*"

"I have to admit I never met another person with that name."

Gabriella giggled. "*Bon!* I like you Missouri Rothman. I'm glad you're my roommate and not one of those young, immature – what do you call them? – twenty-somethings?"

"Yes, but why is that?"

"Because all they want and all they think about is Italian men and how to attract them," she said, her lower lip extending out in a pout. "I am here for serious studying, not to chase the men. What about you, Missouri?"

"Absolutely not! I'm here to learn classical drawing and painting techniques."

"Just how mature are you?"

"Excuse me?"

"I'm 48 years old. And you?"

"I'm 51."

"*C'est pas vrai!* I think early forties. Have you had a face lift? My friend Cheri told me Americans have cosmetic surgery when they are teenagers so they won't ever look old."

Missouri shook her head and stood up. "I've never had any kind of cosmetic surgery and I don't know anyone who has." Missouri stretched her arms overhead. "Now that I have my second wind, you can point me in the direction of my room. I need to keep moving before I drop from exhaustion."

• • • • •

The bedroom contained two twin beds, two desks with chairs, and two armoires. Missouri hauled her suitcase over to the only unmade bed. She paused to look out one of two dark-green wooden-shuttered windows. Three stories down, pedestrians walked up and down the narrow alleyway. For one second, Missouri considered collapsing on top of the mattress for a "disco" nap – a 30-minute nap like her sons used to take before going out for an evening of bar-crawling – but quickly reconsidered her really bad idea. She sighed and began unpacking.

An hour later when Missouri wandered into the kitchen, Gabriella was sliding what she called a spinach *frittata* onto a platter. "You've been here long enough to learn Italian cooking?" asked Missouri, sitting down at the table.

Gabriella poured two glasses of *chiaretto*. "This is a nice rosé wine. I hope you like it." She sat down and pointed to the *frittata*. "This is nothing more than a twist on the French *omelette*. Every dish in Italy is simply a version of a French one."

Missouri took a bite of her Italian *omelette*. "Mmmmm. Gabriella, this is very good." She took a second bite. "Love the fresh mushrooms and spinach. And that cheese. Yummy!"

"French cheese is better, but this *pecorina* I picked up at the Mercato Centrale isn't half bad."

After the kitchen was clean, Gabriella insisted that Missouri go with her to a coffee bar. "You'll love it, *ma chérie*. It's what all the Italians do in the evening. Come with me and soak up some culture."

Just off the Via de Guicciardini near the Ponte Vecchio, Gabriella steered Missouri towards a small coffee bar. She commandeered a small outside table and pulled Missouri down into a chair. "From here we can watch the tourists walk by," she explained and ordered *caffe latte* for Missouri and an *espresso* for herself. "Occasionally, you can catch some street entertainment."

No sooner were the words out of her mouth than a strolling guitarist walked by crooning Italian love songs. A young boy around eight years old followed behind him with a woolen cap for donations. "*Grazie*," he called out as passers-by threw in their Euro change.

By the time she had finished her *latte*, Missouri felt very relaxed. If this was what evenings in Florence were going to be like, then she had much to look forward to. She sighed contentedly and leaned back in her seat.

· · · · ·

The days leading up to the beginning of classes were a blur for Missouri. She had orientation sessions and registration and meetings, meetings, meetings. In between, Gabriella gave her a map and helped her find her way around to the important sites: the open-air market, Zecchi's art supply store, art studios, faculty offices, the closest grocery store or *le supermercato*, and the nearest pharmacy or *la farmacia*. She found the tourist spots wandering around on her own when she left the Oltrarno area and crossed the Ponte Vecchio to see old historic Florence on the north side of the River Arno.

Ponte Vecchio, according to Missouri's guide book, was the oldest bridge in Florence. Built in 1345, it was the only bridge not destroyed during World War II because the townspeople ran out on the bridge and begged the Germans not to blow it up. The bridge was originally home to butchers, tanners and blacksmiths, who used the river as a garbage dump until 1595, when Duke Ferdinando I had them evicted because of the noise and stench. After buildings on the bridge were cleaned up and rebuilt, goldsmiths moved in and to this day shops lining and overhanging the bridge continue to specialize in new and antique jewelry.

Missouri halted halfway across the bridge to admire the river view, street performers, portrait painters and street traders. From her vantage point she could see nearly all of the Corridoio Vasariano, an elevated corridor built in 1565 to link the Palazzo Vecchio to the Palazzo Pitti, thus allowing members of the Medici family to move between palaces without walking the dirty streets below and mixing with the peasants. Also in the middle of the bridge, Missouri found a bust of Benvenuto Cellini, the most famous of all Florentine goldsmiths.

Walking slowly, she paused in front of show windows on the bridge to admire gold and silver jewelry – bracelets, necklaces, rings and brooches – with cameos, pearls and precious stones. She was amazed to find so much expensive jewelry in one spot.

On the north bank of the Arno, Missouri turned right along the river and the Lungarno D. Archbusieri, pausing occasionally to peer over the old stone wall at the water below and the buildings on the opposite side of the river. The area was teeming with tourists by the time she reached the Piazzle Vegli Uffizi, the cobblestone passageway leading to the world's oldest art gallery. The Uffizi, built in the late 1500s as office space for Duke Cosimo I's administration, was used by his heirs as a place to display the Medici family art treasures.

Missouri stood in the *piazzale* and looked at the long, long line of tourists and visitors waiting patiently to enter the famous museum. Gabrielle told her that during the height of tourist season, some people waited in line for hours. Those visitors who were enlightened, purchased dated admission tickets ahead of time at the Pitti Palace. A second, much shorter line was available for them. Sort of like having a Fast Pass at a Disney theme park, Missouri decided and smiled to herself.

When Missouri first heard that her art class would be visiting the Uffizi, she broke out in goose bumps. The closest she had come to seeing a real art museum was attending a special exhibition at the university's small art museum. Even when she and Doyle had lived in Naples and visited Rome, Doyle scoffed at the idea of seeing any art museums. But Missouri did see a few classical Roman statues lying around the ruins.

Missouri turned reluctantly away from the Uffizi and headed toward the Palazzo Vecchio or Old Palace, which was built in 1322, but was still used for its original purpose as a town hall. A huge bell in its tall tower alerted the citizens to meetings or warned them about fire, flood or an enemy attack. Inside, the guide book explained, the *palazzo* still retained its medieval appearance.

Outside the entrance of the *palazzo* stood a copy of Michelangelo's famous statue of "David." The original marble colossal nude "David," created in 1504, stood in front of the Palazzo Vecchio until 1873, when it was moved inside the Galleria dell'Academy to protect it from the weather and pollution. If this insignificant copy looked half as good as the real thing, then Missouri thought she'd probably swoon when she finally saw it.

Across from "David," Missouri recognized the Loggia dei Lanzi from a picture in her art history book. The back wall of the 14th century covered porch was lined with ancient Roman statues of priestesses. But in the front of the loggia stood several significant statues including Cellini's bronze statue "Perseus" and Giambologna's famous "Rape of the Sabine Women," carved from a single block of flawed marble. Missouri looked at the "Sabine Women" from every angle and marveled at the writhing figures and the woman's terrified expression.

Like many piazzas throughout Italy, the Piazza della Signoria had a fountain. Ammannati's Mannerist fountain depicted a larger-than-life nude statue of King Neptune – the Roman sea god – surrounded by water nymphs. The fountain itself, built in 1575, commemorated Tuscan naval victories.

After resting on the edge of the fountain for a few minutes and observing hordes of excited tourists snapping photos with cell phones and cameras, Missouri crossed the huge *pizzale* to the Via dei Calzaiuoli, a major pedestrian passageway that led directly to the Duomo. She only stopped twice as she wove in and out of the crowd of people: once, to buy a cone of hazelnut *gelato* – rich, creamy Italian ice cream – and a second time in front of the Disney Store, where

Mickey and Minnie beckoned her to enter and open her wallet. She laughed out loud as two little girls, fists wrapped around their mother's skirt, tugged the woman towards the store's door. Kids are the same no matter what country they live in, she noticed.

The size and exquisiteness of the Duomo – *Santa Maria del Fiore* – and its campanile and baptistry caught Missouri by surprise. The 13th century cathedral, which was built on top of the 4th-century church of *Santa Reparata* (its remains were in the crypt of the Duomo), had a Neo-Gothic green, white and pink marble façade that was not added until the 1870s. Gabriella told Missouri that the top of the towering orange-red brick dome, Brunelleschi's revolutionary achievement, was built without scaffolding. Anyone willing to climb the 463 steps to the top was rewarded with a spectacular view of the city. Missouri looked at the long, long line of waiting tourists and elected to pass up this opportunity. She knew her knees would thank her.

In backing up to get a better view of the Duomo, Missouri nearly collided with a horse and carriage. "*Scusi! Scusi!*" she cried out – more so to the poor horse, than to the red-faced, frowning driver spouting angry Italian words at her. She scurried out of the way of the horse, actually relieved that her Italian was not good enough to understand what he was yelling at her. Oh bother, she thought wearily as she made her way back towards Oltrarno and the safety of her apartment. She was starting to realize that living in Florence was definitely going to have its ups and downs.

Chapter Nine

Missouri's teacher for Introduction to Drawing and Painting in the Classical Style was an American. This surprised her. He was definitely not what she'd been expecting. Much younger than she had anticipated. Not much older than her son Michael, she decided, as she watched him enter the classroom. His light brown hair, peppered with grey, was parted down the center and brushed the tops of his ears on the sides, his collar in the back and his eyes in the front. He was stocky and muscular, with the unkempt, unshaved look she really didn't care for, but which was favored by her son Cody and his friends.

"*Buongiorno*," he greeted the class. "*Mi chiamo*, David Harris." Then he pulled out a pair of half-frame reading glasses and began calling the roll. Azure blue eyes peered intently over the top of his glasses at Missouri as she responded to her name. He pushed his hair back out of his eyes with his fingers. Was it only her imagination or had he paused briefly before continuing with the next name?

David Harris removed his reading glasses, carefully folded and placed them in his pocket and seemed to study each of the twelve faces in his new class. Missouri looked around, too. She saw a very diverse group, age-wise and nationality-wise. She and Gabriella appeared to be the only older students in the class. The remaining students were from Canada, Great Britain, Australia, South Africa and the United States. How fresh and eager everyone looked, she thought. Here they were in Florence for an educational experience and an opportunity to immerse themselves in the Italian history, culture, language and lifestyle. Missouri remembered what Ron told her – that one could not realize or comprehend how studying on Italian soil would shape and change the rest of one's life and influence one's art. Missouri was glad that she made the journey to Florence to find out. To hell with Doyle.

•   •   •   •   •

Unlike most classes at the university, classes at the Academy of Art met every weekday. In the morning, Missouri had a class in Italian language and culture, followed by Italian art history. After a two-hour break for lunch, Missouri spent all afternoon and evening in her studio class. At the end of the day, Gabriella and Missouri often shared a small evening meal at their apartment to conserve money, but usually went out afterwards to chat with other students over *caffe latte* or *espresso* or *cappucino*.

Missouri loved Saturdays. That was the day students toured museums and churches throughout Florence. In art history classes at American universities, students had to be content with slide presentations of artwork, but in Florence, students saw actual works by famous artists. The first Saturday field trip was to the Uffizi to study figures in Botticelli's "Birth of Venus" and "Primavera" and in Fra Filippo Lippi's "Madonna and Child with Angels."

The night before the museum visit, Missouri was so excited she could not sleep. Once inside the Uffizi, she wanted to enter the first room and slowly absorb each piece of art one by one, but the class assignment came first, and Missouri knew she would return to the Uffizi many more times.

When Missouri finally stood in front of the "Birth of Venus," she stared in awe for a long time before pulling out her sketchbook and pencil. She became so absorbed in drawing the face of Venus that she was not aware of David standing behind her until he spoke. "You seem to have a flair for faces, Mrs. Rothman. Or may I call you Missouri?"

His voice startled her and she dropped her sketchbook, which had been balanced on the palm of her left hand. David bent over and retrieved the sketchbook off of the marble floor. "Thank you," she said, her cheeks burning as she accepted the sketchbook from her teacher.

"I'm sorry," he said with a smile. "I didn't mean to sneak up and scare you."

Missouri shook her head as she thumbed through the pages in her sketchbook to find the right spot. "No, it wasn't your fault." She looked into his blue eyes and swallowed hard. "I...uh...was concentrating on my drawing. I didn't know you were back there."

"So I noticed, and I understand perfectly," he said not moving. "I remember my first trip to the Uffizi as a student."

She took in a long breath. "It's like more visual stimulation than one person can handle," she said without thinking. Then she felt like an idiot and wished she'd said something more intelligent.

But David laughed. "That's a good way to describe it. I know exactly what you mean."

"Please, don't laugh at me. This is my first art museum and I'm simply overwhelmed."

David's face registered surprise. "You've never before been to an art museum?"

"Only the small art museum at the university." Missouri grimaced. She couldn't believe she'd admitted that to her teacher. Now he really would think she was an idiot.

"I'm quite dumbfounded, Mrs. Rothman, but very glad we've been able to rectify that for you." He smiled at her. "You're from the University of Georgia, aren't you? The Lamar Dodd School of Art?"

Missouri blinked. "Yes and yes."

"Excuse me?" he asked, puzzled.

"Yes, I'm from Georgia and yes, you may call me Missouri."

He chuckled softly. "Okay, Missouri. I don't get too many nontraditional students like you and Gabriella."

"Is that good or bad?"

"I find that nontraditional students tend to take their work more seriously than most of the younger ones."

"Because we're mature and well seasoned?"

"Because you've experienced more of life and it shows in your work."

Missouri turned back to sketching Venus' wavy hair. "In that case, is it all right for a nontraditional student to call her professor by his first name?"

He smiled. "Yes, Missouri, of course, but only outside of class."

"Good." She glanced at him. "I'm still adjusting to having teachers who are barely older than my sons."

"Just how old do you think I am?"

"Oh, mmmmmmmmmm." She grimaced. She didn't want to make such a bad guess that he would be annoyed. She crossed her fingers. "Thirty-five, maybe?"

He chuckled, again. "Actually, I'm forty-two. About the same age as you, right?"

"Oh, yeah, that's me all right." She looked back at her sketch, "I'm right around there, too."

•   •   •   •   •

"*Mon dieu, chérie!*" exclaimed Gabriella when Missouri told her about her conversation with David. "*Je ne comprends pas!* Why not just tell him the truth? When you reach our age, what does it matter?"

Missouri collapsed on the sofa next to Gabriella. She sighed. "I don't know. I just couldn't admit that I'm about ten years older than him."

Gabriella wrinkled her forehead and leaned toward Missouri. "Perhaps you find Monsieur Harris a teeny bit attractive, *non?*"

Missouri closed her eyes and waved her hand. "Oh, piffle...of course, he's an attractive man. I'm old, not blind." Maybe that's what happened to Doyle, she thought. He wasn't blind when it came to a pretty young woman – even if she were 20 years younger.

"Perhaps *madame* does not want Monsieur Harris to know she is an older woman, *n'est-ce pas?*"

Missouri opened one eye and then the other and sat up, glaring at Gabriella, who was starting to giggle. Soon they were both rolling on the couch and laughing loudly like a pair of high school girls. Finally, Missouri stopped and wiped her eyes. "Goodness Miss Agnes," she muttered. "I haven't acted this silly about a male teacher since high school."

"*Oui,*" agreed Gabriella, sighing happily. "I know what you say. But this feels good, yes?"

"Yes," she said with a splutter and a laugh.

"By the way, I have some mail for you." Gabriella reached into her book bag, pulled out several letters and handed them to Missouri.

Missouri took them eagerly and quickly read the return addresses. "Happy day," she exclaimed. "I have letters from both my sons. How did you do?"

"I have one from *ma mère* and another from my male friend Jean Philippe. And what about your third letter?"

"That's...uh...from my ex," she replied, setting it aside.

Gabriella nodded. They sat in silence, opening and quietly reading their connections and lifelines to home. "Good news?" asked Gabriella, as Missouri returned Michael's and Cody's letters to their envelopes.

"My youngest, Cody, sold a poem to a poetry magazine, and Michael just got promoted."

"That's great!" Gabriella said.

"Not really. They both want me to return home."

"What about the letter from your ex?"

Missouri reluctantly opened Doyle's letter, which had been written on his computer and printed out on his Hewlett Packard DeskJet using his favorite Garamond Condensed font. She read the first couple of sentences, then angrily wadded it up and threw it across the room.

"*Qu'est-ce qui ne va pas*? Did he write bad thing?" asked a concerned Gabriella.

"He wants me to go home and help him put our marriage back together."

"And this...this you do not want?"

Missouri sat back and sighed. "What I want right now is to continue my studies here in Florence. As for trying to pull my marriage back together? I simply don't know if that's what I want."

· · · · ·

At the end of class on Wednesday, David announced that on Saturday, the class would meet at 8 a.m. in the Piazza di Santa Felicita at the Ponte Vecchio for an all-day field trip to San Miniato al Monte. "Wear your good hiking shoes, comfortable clothes and a hat with a brim. Pack plenty of water, food, art supplies, and something to sit on," he said. "The view of Florence is magnificent. We'll walk up, do our thing and the school van will meet us mid-afternoon for the trip back."

The generously proportioned young man from Australia raised his hand. "I say, mate, couldn't we ride up and walk down?"

"Trust me when I say you will not want a two-hour walk back."

"Why's that, mate?"

Missouri wanted to know, too, but she wasn't going to ask. She appreciated the young man's courage.

"Because you will be tired, it will be hot by mid-afternoon, and I'm not carrying you on my back if you pass out."

Muffled laughter came from the back corner of the classroom where the four Canadians were sitting.

"Is this an optional field trip, mate?"

"No, mate, it isn't."

· · · · ·

By the time David arrived at the *piazza*, the entire class was accounted for and ready to depart. He greeted them enthusiastically and led the way up the Via de

Bardi, along the river, to the Piazza de Mozzi and the palazzo built of recycled medieval and Renaissance masonry. Gabriella and Missouri naturally fell to the back of the group. Not because they were older and slower, Missouri told herself, but because there was so much to see along the way. Gabriella, who was enrolled in a photography class, stopped about every 10 feet to take a photo.

From the Piazza de Mozzi, the group hiked along the Via de San Niccolo, past the San Miniato archway and the 14th century San Niccolo gateway in the old city wall dating from 1258. When Missouri and Gabriella caught up with their classmates, they were sprawled in the shade resting. David rose to his feet. "Come on, ladies. Don't sit down. We're making a right hand turn here and I don't want to lose anyone." David pointed up the steep stone steps. "Our final destination lies at the top."

The mate from Australia, who already was warm and sweaty, groaned softly and took a long swig of water from his two-liter bottle. "It looks quite steep," he said. The other students nodded in agreement.

David smiled. "What are you, a bunch of wussies?" He patted the Australian on his back. "You can do it, mate, and you'll be thanking me at the top."

With a tree trunk for support, the Australian pulled himself to a standing position. Shaking his head, he mumbled softly, "If you say so, mate," and began slowly making his way up the steps. Grumbling, the others followed.

"*Un moment*, Monsieur Harris," called out Gabriella.

David paused and turned to face her. "What is it?"

"We haven't had time to rest," Missouri said.

"You'll be fine, ladies. You're both fit, you'll make it," he said, starting up the steps.

Missouri and Gabriella looked at each other, rolled their eyes and followed after the group, one foot in front of the other. It didn't take too many steps before Missouri was breathing hard, and each step was more difficult than the other. "This is too much," she said to no one in particular.

David stopped his upward climb and turned around when Gabriella passed him. He looked at Missouri, who had paused to catch her breath. "Come on, come on. Don't stop now. We're almost to the top." He reached down and offered her his hand.

"You told me that half an hour ago," she puffed, grabbing his hand.

He laughed. "I was trying to encourage you to keep going. It must have worked or you wouldn't have gotten this far."

Missouri let David help her up a few more steep steps, then the path gave way to a flat paved area – the Piazzale Michelangelo. Here a copy of Michelangelo's *David* towered above the asphalt parking lot, which was full of tourists, cars, vans, busses, souvenir stands and artists sitting under umbrellas with their creative works on display.

Missouri started toward a woman who was working with watercolors, but David grabbed her arm and pointed to the edge of the parking lot. "Over here, Missouri. This is what you came for."Missouri followed David to the edge of the *piazzale* where the rest of the class was standing and let out a breath that closely resembled a muted squeal. There below was a mind-blowing view of Florence and the River Arno. Sticking out prominently above the Florence skyline were the great Duomo with its huge orange-red dome, the campanile of the Palazzo Vecchio and the magnificent gothic church of Santa Croce. The River Arno ran from left to right like a silvery blue ribbon, interrupted by the Ponte Vecchio and other bridges.

Missouri stood next to David and a stone wall, warm from the afternoon Tuscan sun. Suddenly, all the doubts she'd had after reading letters from Doyle and her sons melted away. She unslung the painter's bag from her shoulder and pulled out paper, brushes, watercolors and water bottle. She was going to sit here by the wall and paint this intoxicating scene. This was the right thing for Missouri Rothman to do.

Chapter Ten

On Friday night, Gabriella and Missouri were in their favorite *caffè* bar near the Ponte Vecchio when David ambled in. Gabriella was nursing a *cappuccino*, while Missouri was indulging in a *cioccolato con panna*, which was much thicker than American hot chocolate and served with a big dollop of whipped cream. Four students at an adjacent table had discovered Kinder chocolate eggs, which were sold throughout the world, but not in the USA — where they had been banned as a choking hazard. Inside each hollow egg was a yellow plastic "yolk" filled with a colorful miniature toy – some assembly required. The students, who seemed to be addicted to the toys, had tired of eating the chocolate and were trying unsuccessfully to give it away to other patrons in the *caffè* bar.

David stopped and chatted with the chocolate overloaded students, accepting a few pieces of chocolate egg and admiring the growing assortment of tiny toys: fantasy creatures, vehicles of various types, humanoid figures and other creations. Swallowing a final mouthful of chocolate, David turned toward Missouri and Gabriella and smiled.

"*Buonasera, Signore,*" he greeted them. "May I join you?"

"*Piacere,*" responded Missouri. "We would be pleased."

"*Bien sûr,*" said Gabriella. "We mature women never turn down an opportunity to keep company with an attractive man." She winked at Missouri.

"Whoa, just a minute now," exclaimed David. "What is all that winking about?" He sat down across the table from Missouri.

"*Je ne sais pas,*" Gabriella answered innocently. "I know not what you mean, Monsieur Harris."

David half-rose from his chair. "I think I'll go sit somewhere else."

Gabriella stood and pushed him down into the chair. "*Mais non, Monsieur.* You stay. I'm leaving to phone my sister. She's taking a holiday in Nice and today's her birthday." She blew a kiss in Missouri's direction.

"See you in a little bit, Gabby," Missouri called out after her.

"*Ciao*, Gabby," said David. Then he turned his attention to Missouri. "She really does have a sister on holiday in Nice, right? It wasn't just a ploy to leave us alone, was it?"

Missouri looked at him and smiled, then averted her eyes by taking a sip of her hot chocolate. "Yes and yes," she mumbled and was relieved to hear him laugh.

For several minutes David sat quietly, smiling and watching Missouri. Missouri continued to sip her chocolate, while watching him covertly from beneath her lashes. She wondered why he was sitting there with such a dopey expression on his face.

"Don't you want a cup of coffee or something?" she finally asked, setting aside her cup and looking questioningly at him.

He shook his head. "No, thank you, I've had my evening coffee already. I really came in here to ask you a question."

Missouri sat up straight in her chair. "Class-related or personal?"

"I'd call it personal, I guess," he said, raising his eyebrows in question. "Is that all right?"

Her mouth twitched slightly. What personal question could he possibly want to ask her? "Ask away. But I'm not promising you'll get an answer."

David leaned forward across the table and lowered his voice.

"I'm inviting you to my place for dinner tomorrow night."

She looked up in surprise. "You cook?"

"Come judge for yourself."

Missouri wasn't sure how to respond. Was it appropriate for a student to go to her professor's home for dinner?

"I'm cooking Italian...*bruschetta...risotto di asparagi...salmone in camicia...tiramisu...*" he rattled off his dinner menu.

On the other hand, she thought, she did enjoy his company and would like to get to know him better. It wasn't like she was young and impressionable. She continued to mull over the pros and cons in her mind.

"This is all on the up and up," he continued after noticing her hesitation. "I have a policy against seducing my female students."

She thought he was smiling like a young boy trying to coax a pretty girl to hold his prize frog. She smiled back. Dang it all, what was she afraid of? "Okay," she agreed, "but only if I can bring a bottle of wine."

"Agreed. Seven o'clock okay for you?"

"Yes," she replied, feeling somewhat giddy. Ahh, Missouri, she fussed at herself, do you know what you're doing? No, she didn't, but she needed to do this as she continued to evolve into a new woman. What could be the harm?

•   •   •   •   •

Not only did Gabriella help Missouri select the wine, a nice Vernaccia di San Gimignano, she also loaned her a Parisian designer dress -- soft, flowing, forest green silk, which went well with her auburn hair and showed off her curves. Then Gabriella brushed her side curls up on top of her head and pinned them in place with an antique silver hair comb, shaped like a butterfly. She stepped back to admire her creation. "*Zut! Magnifique*! Monsieur Harris will not be able to take his eyes off you."

Missouri blushed with excitement. "Don't make trouble, Gabby. It's just dinner."

"*Mais oui, bien sûr.*"

"Don't be ridiculous, Gabby...he's young enough to be my son."

"*Mais non*! He's barely ten years younger than you."

"Still a child compared to me."

"Where *l'amour* is in the picture, age does not matter."

"You're an impossible romantic." Missouri grabbed her purse and wine and headed to the door. "Don't wait up for me."

•   •   •   •   •

Missouri took a bite of the *bruschetta* and closed her eyes to better savor the blended flavors of crusty bread, olive oil, garlic, basil, oregano, chopped tomato, freshly grated romano – toasted under the broiler. "Mmmmmm! This is yummy, David."

"Do you have to sound so surprised?"

"I'm sorry. It's just that my husband..." She stopped, cringed and glanced down at a bit of tomato that had fallen to her plate. "My ex-husband, that is, couldn't boil water without instructions and only one of my sons knows how to use pots and pans to cook.

David pushed back from the table and stood up. "Most men probably don't see a need to cook if there's a woman around to fill that job description. I was that way, too. But after my wife died, I started cooking so I wouldn't eat a lot of fast food." David stepped to the stove and returned with two servings of steaming *risotto*.

"I'm sorry about your wife. How long has it been?" asked Missouri. Now she understood why David didn't have a wedding band. She thought he might have been divorced.

"About three years ago. Breast cancer."

"How awful. How many years were you married?"

"Fifteen."

"Children?"

David shook his head. "No, afraid not. We both wanted children. It just didn't happen for us. We'd turned in our paperwork and were approved to adopt about the time Aurelia became sick."

"Aurelia? Was she Italian?"

"Yes, I met her here in Florence about twenty years ago when I came over here to study and find myself."

"And did you find yourself?"

"I found myself, and fell in love with Italy, the Italian people and Aurelia, whom I wed and took back to America. We settled into a fifth floor walk-up apartment in Greenwich Village. After finishing my MFA at Pratt Institute, I went to work at the New York Metropolitan Museum of Art as a curator, and Aurelia became an art teacher at a private school."

Missouri took a bite of the asparagus *risotto*. David poured her more wine. "David, this rice dish is quite delicious, creamy and full of flavor."

"Thank you. The trick is to cook it very slowly, adding the hot chicken broth a little at a time until..." he kissed the tips of his fingers "...it is melt-in-your-mouth perfect."

"You must give me the recipe. I'd like to try making it."

"The recipe is yours."

"Thanks. Now I want to hear more about your life in New York. I always thought that would be a fun place to live and work."

"As I look back, I think we led an idyllic life. Aurelia sculpted outside of teaching, while I became known in the New York art scene for my sensual nude female figures."

"Nudes? You paint nudes?"

"Not any more. I haven't felt like painting since Aurelia died."

"It must have been hard on Aurelia to give up her family and Italian culture to move to America."

"Yes, she did get homesick occasionally. But every other year, we returned to Italy to visit Aurelia's family in Florence and her old friends. We'd eat lots of traditional Italian meals and drink our favorite Tuscan wines that we couldn't find in New York. It was a good life. Then five years ago, Aurelia was diagnosed with breast cancer. She died after a two-year battle. I was so heartsick and depressed that I had to leave New York. I accepted a teaching position at the Academy, returning to the city that Aurelia and I both loved, looking for consolation and healing."

"And did you find it? Consolation and healing?"

He swallowed hard. "Each year is easier than the one before."

Missouri could hear the emotion in his voice. "I'm sure it hasn't been easy."

David took a sip of wine. "Why don't you tell me about this ex-husband of yours. Why did you divorce him?"

Missouri looked down at her plate. She hesitated to answer him. No one before had asked her that question. What could she say? That Doyle wanted to swap his old, ugly fat wife for a sweet young thing?

"I'm sorry, Missouri." He reached out for her hand. "My question was out of line. It's none of my business. I apologize."

Missouri pulled her hands into her lap. "No need to apologize," she said softly, glancing at him. His face was full of concern. "Doyle wanted the divorce, not me. He...uh...fell in love with a younger woman." Her voice trailed off as her throat tightened. She couldn't believe thinking about it still hurt and it'd been over a year now. When was she going to be over it? "I'm sorry, I don't mean to be so emotional. It's absolutely ridiculous. I really have tried to put it behind me."

"I understand perfectly. It's been three years since Aurelia died and anything – a thought, a smell, a sight – can trigger my grief instantly."

"Thanks for understanding." They ate without talking for about a minute, then Missouri broke the silence. "I find it interesting that you do nudes."

"Why is that?" David asked, scooping poached salmon onto her plate.

"I have several books on Andrew Wyeth at home and I love his nudes much better than his landscapes. One day I'd like to go to that museum in Rockport, Maine, and see some of his nudes in real life."

"His Helga nudes?"

"Those are okay, but my favorites are the ones he did of Siri."

"You do realize he started painting her when she was only 15 years old?"

"Yes, I read that. Do you have favorites yourself?"

"Modigliani.

Missouri repeated the name several times. "I'm not familiar with that name. Italian, of course?"

"He was very talented, but he died very young at the age of 36 years."

"Recently?"

David laughed. "Hardly!"

"Are you laughing at me, again?" Missouri felt hurt and stupid. "I realize I'm not as knowledgeable about art and artists as the other students, but I'm working very hard to overcome my ignorance."

David's smile disappeared. "I'm sorry. Because he's my favorite and I know so much about him, I assume wrongly that everyone else does, too." He finished off his glass of wine. "Would you be interested in hearing more about Amedeo Modigliani?"

"Please" she answered quietly, wishing she was more knowledgeable about artists. The more she learned, the more she realized how little she knew.

"I have several books on him that you can read, if you're interested, but here are the highlights of his short life: Amedeo Modigliani was born in 1884 in Livorno, Italy, to a Jewish family. After a rough childhood, he studied art in Florence, Venice and Paris. He had bad health, including bouts with typhoid fever and tuberculosis. Also, he was a heavy smoker, drinker and hashish user. But he gained a wide reputation for his portraits. He tried sculpting with stone for a few years, followed by a year painting nudes. He began a relationship with Jeanne Hebuterne and they had a daughter in 1918. He became ill in 1919, and died penniless in Paris in 1920. I guess you'd say he was one of those Parisian avant-garde artists of Montmartre and Montparnasse."

"Some of that sounds familiar," said Missouri thoughtfully. "He wasn't the artist who painted all the women with long noses and swan-like necks, was he?"

"Yes, he's the one."

She smiled with relief that she wasn't as stupid as she thought. "Yes, I remember seeing something about him on public television. Didn't his pregnant girlfriend kill herself after he died?"

"Yes, pregnant with their second child."

"That's really sad. You must show me pictures of his nudes. I bet I would like them."

"How about some coffee and *tiramisu*?" David asked.

During the rest of the meal, David reminisced about his time as an art student in Florence. Missouri talked about her sons Michael and Cody, and her years caring for her father-in-law. David explained why after Aurelia's death he felt it necessary to quit his job and return to Florence, a city they both loved. And finally Missouri was able to share with David the shock and hurt she felt when Doyle divorced her, her months of despair and her struggle to start a new life. Missouri was amazed at how easy it was to talk to David about such personal aspects of her life.

Missouri finished her *caffè latte* and pushed back from the table. "David, it's getting late. I really must go. Thank you so much for the home-cooked meal and entertaining dinner conversation. I also enjoyed getting to know you."

David wrapped her sweater around her shoulders and steered her toward the door. "I'll walk you back to your apartment."

"Oh, no, please. It's not that far," she protested.

David gave her a gentle nudge toward the door and followed her out. "The escort service comes free with dinner. That's your reward for eating my cooking."

• • • • •

Missouri's apartment was only four blocks from David's. The shortest route was through narrow, dark streets with no sidewalks. Only a handful of people passed them during their walk. Suddenly a speeding scooter zoomed around a corner, catching them off-guard. In her efforts to get out of the way, Missouri tripped on a cobblestone. David grabbed her upper arms protectively and prevented her from falling on her face.

"See? Aren't you glad you signed up for the Harris Escort Service?" he asked charmingly.

Missouri couldn't help but laugh. "Yes, I'm grateful. You saved me from a nasty fall."

David reached out and took her left hand in his right. Instinctively, she tried to pull back, but he tightened his grasp. "Do you have a problem with me holding your hand?"

Missouri swallowed hard. "No," she said softly. The last man who wanted to hold her hand was Doyle. David wasn't Doyle. It was okay, she told herself. David relaxed his hold and this time she didn't pull away.

At the entranceway to her building, Missouri thanked David, again, for dinner. "It was the best Italian food I've ever had – impressive and delicious," she told him.

"For a man?" he teased her.

"For anyone. Also, I enjoyed getting to know you better."

"That goes for me, too."

"Good night, David. *Ciao*!" Missouri unlocked the iron gate at the bottom of the steps and went inside.

"Wait!" David called out. From the other side of the metal bars, he said, "I want to see you, again."

Missouri halted on the staircase. "But David, we'll see each other in class on Monday."

"How about sooner – like tomorrow?" he asked. She didn't reply immediately. "I'm thinking a picnic in Boboli Gardens. I'll make *panini* with vine-ripe tomatoes and thick slices of buffalo mozzarella."

She looked down at the ancient stone steps worn down in the center from more than 800 years of use. "I don't know, David. I need to get some sketching done." She hesitated.

"Bring your sketchbook. I know a great spot under some shade trees with a fantastic view."

She glanced at him with interest. "Really?"

"Really. Say yes."

"Oh, okay. Yes."

"Excellent! I'll meet you in front of the Pitti Palace at noon." David turned to leave.

"Okay, but there's something I have to tell you first." David stopped and faced her. "Something about me that you need to know."

He stepped closer to the gate. "What's that?"

"I'm...uh...I'm much older than you are. I'm over 50 years old." She cringed. That sounded like she was totally ancient, she thought.

He looked at her sternly. She felt her heart beat faster. Then he smirked impishly. "I have a confession to make, too: I already know that. I looked it up in your academic record. *Ci vediamo domani*!" He bowed, blew her a kiss and then he was gone, leaving Missouri standing with her mouth agape.

•   •   •   •   •

When Missouri arrived at the Pitti Palace at noon, David was nowhere to be seen. She sat on the wall out front and waited. From the entrance to the palace, the stone-covered courtyard sloped steeply down to the Piazza de Pitti and the Via de Guicciardini. Singles, couples and families, tourists and townspeople, sat or reclined in the sun, enjoying their Sunday afternoon. Missouri was reminded of pleasant afternoons in Athens when the university students would plop down all over the North Quadrangle and Herty Field, reading, napping, eating and visiting with friends. But she couldn't help but feel the lush green grass on the UGA campus was a whole lot softer and more comfortable than these Italian stones.

"Sorry I'm late," gasped an out-of-breath David behind her. "I had to stop along the way for a bottle of wine."

Missouri saw that David's face glistened with perspiration. "No problem," she said, gesturing toward the sun-soaking individuals. "I've been enjoying the sights."

As they walked through the Boboli Gardens behind the Pitti Palace, David explained that the gardens were laid out for the Medici family after they bought the *palazzo* in 1549. "They call this stylized Renaissance gardening. It was opened to the public in 1766."

Strolling down gravel paths, Missouri observed the box hedges, clipped into symmetrical geometric patterns, then wilder groves of holly and cypress trees, flowering shrubs, ponds and fountains, classic statues and vistas of Florence. Finally the path they were on opened up into a grassy quadrangle with a large Roman face sculpture. Downhill from there, at the edge of the grass were several park benches with – as David had promised – a magnificent view of the city.

"David, it's awesome!" Missouri scampered over to one of the benches and sat down. She immediately pulled out her leather-bound sketchbook and pencil and went to work.

David grinned at her and shook his head. He carefully wriggled the backpack he was carrying off his shoulders and sat down beside her. "Does this view live up to your expectations?" he asked, unzipping the largest section of his backpack.

"Absolutely." On the space between them, David spread out a dark cotton cloth and carefully covered it with *panini* sandwiches, a carton of seafood pasta salad, a container of olives, two plastic glasses and a bottle of white wine.

David sprawled back on the bench and devoured a crusty sandwich with tomato oozing out the sides. He watched Missouri nibble and sketch at the same time. "How can you do that?" he asked, while gingerly spitting an olive seed into a nearby bush.

"It's the so-little-time student syndrome," she replied deadpan. "Our art professors have these impossible expectations and we students have so little time to fulfill and meet these expectations, that we often have no time to eat a proper meal." She watched in satisfaction the sheepish grin on David's face.

Finished with lunch and the wine, which he drank most of, David put the leftovers away. From the smaller front pouch, he pulled out a bottle of *Vino Santo* and a box of *biscotti*. He opened the cookies and filled their glasses. Missouri continued to draw, taking an occasional sip of the strong, sweet wine and small bites of the hard cookie. Her head was feeling oozy from the *San Grigio*, so she only had one glass of the new bottle. David poured himself more.

Finally, Missouri shut her sketchbook and put away her pencils. She relaxed against the back of the bench and stretched to loosen the muscles in her neck and shoulders, squeezing her shoulders with opposite hands. "Here, let me," offered David as he reached over and gently began massaging her shoulders and neck.

At first Missouri felt uncomfortable. Doyle was the only man who had ever massaged her, and he only did it to loosen her up prior to sex. But it felt so good, she didn't want David to stop. "Ahhh, yes..." She could feel the stress melt away. He was better than Magic. "That really feels good. I'd let you do this all day, but I need to focus on my drawings."

David dropped his hands. "I need to talk to your teachers. Let them know they are working you too hard."

"Yeah, you do that. Make sure you start with my drawing instructor. He's the worst."

"I'll do that. Meanwhile, how about another *biscotti*?" He pushed one into her mouth.

She pulled the cookie out. "I give up, you're hopeless." Missouri sighed contentedly and leaned back against the bench to savor the view.

David nonchalantly placed his arm along the top of the bench back. "Have you tried dipping your *biscotti* in the wine? That's how the Italians do it." He demonstrated by dunking his in the wine and then into his mouth.

Hesitantly, Missouri did as he suggested and took a bite of the dripping cookie. She leaned back against his arm, closed her eyes and tasted the mixed flavors of cookie and strong sweet wine. "Mmmmm, yummm." She sipped more wine and felt the heat of the alcohol flow down her throat to her stomach.

"This stuff is potent, but good." She leaned close to David and sighed happily as his hand dropped to her shoulder. She felt full of bliss and peace. Of course, she mused, most of this good feeling could probably be attributed to the wine.

David gave her shoulder a squeeze. "Feeling good?"

"Oh, yes," she replied. She looked into his blue eyes and wondered if he wore tinted contacts. "I'm feeling really good."

"I'm feeling lightheaded myself, but I love this *Vino Santo*." He finished a second glass of the sweet wine and poured a third. After finishing that glass, he reached down with his right hand and clasped hers. "There's something I want you to do for me."

"What's that?" she asked, noting how the tone in his voice had turned serious.

He looked off in the distance. "I've not been able to...no, that's not right...I haven't felt like doing any painting since Aurelia died." Missouri squeezed his hand. "It's like I lost any desire to create. Like a light's been extinguished in my head. But now..." David turned his eyes towards her. "Now I think I'm ready to pick up my paint brush and try, again."

"Why, David, that's great. I'm very happy for you," Missouri replied excitedly, her voice rising a few decibels. "I'd love to watch you paint or do you hate having someone look over your shoulder while you work?"

"Not if that someone is you, Missouri." David chuckled and held the bottle out to Missouri. "More?"

"No thank you, my head is already swimming. It doesn't take much wine to make me giddy, and I'm already there. So what happened to make you want to pick up a paint brush, again?"

"Meeting and getting to know you. You are passionate and kind and fun to be around. Your presence in my life has given me back my desire to paint, again." He paused, his eyes locked on hers. "The first thing I want to paint is you."

Missouri swallowed the last of her *Vino Santo*. She smiled. "My portrait?"

"No, I want to paint all of you. The full figure."

"Wearing jeans and a sweater or something more formal? Because I don't have anything dressy."

David smiled and finished off the last of the *Vino Santo*. "Have you forgotten? I don't paint models wearing clothes."

Missouri digested his words slowly. She was feeling a little bit woozy from the wine. Surely she had not heard him right. But something clicked in her brain. Yes, he did tell her he was known for his sensual, nude paintings of women. "You want me to model for you in the nude? You're kidding, right?" She laughed nervously.

David raised an eyebrow, but said nothing.

A quiver of apprehension stirred in her abdomen. "You can't be serious?"

David slid closer to her. "Didn't I tell you that I'm always serious when it comes to my work."

Missouri looked down at her sketch book. Internal warning bells trembled deep inside of her. She leaned forward, pulling away from David's arm. She looked back at him. "First of all, David, I've never modeled for any artist, with or without clothes. Secondly, I'm too old and too fat to start modeling in the buff."

David sighed. "You couldn't be more wrong. Missouri, you are just the kind of model I like to paint. You have that sweet girl-next-door look. Andrew Wyeth's kind of model. I would love to paint you."

She shook her head and stood up. "Andrew Wyeth never painted old, fat women." She laughed to ease the tension and the knot in her stomach.

Looking disappointed, David stood beside her, swaying a little bit. "Missouri, I'm not some sort of sexual pervert. I'm a professional artist who uses nude models. I pay top dollar for my models."

"You don't have to pay me anything because I'm not modeling for you or Andrew Wyeth or Modigliani." She started walking toward the path. It was way past time to leave.

David, a little unsteady on his feet from the wine, followed her. "What if I give the painting to you when I finish? You could hang it up or destroy it?"

Missouri paused and turned to look at him. "But if you give your painting to me, what's in it for you?" She couldn't believe she actually asked that question when she knew she'd never ever consider modeling for him or anyone else.

He laughed, propping himself against a tree trunk. "I can't believe you haven't figured it out." His blue eyes darkened. "I get to see you naked."

Missouri's eyes widened. Her cheeks flushed. She couldn't believe what she heard. Their time together had been perfect. When had it started to go wrong? About the time they had that first glass of the *Vino Santo*. It was obvious to Missouri now that David was drunk. "David, I need to go home and I think you do, too."

David stumbled closer to her. "Only if you come home with me. I'm having too much fun to end it now. What do you say?"

"I'm going home. Period. End of discussion."

Before Missouri could take one step, David grabbed her and kissed her lips. When she tried to pull away, he pulled her up against him. Missouri shoved him away. He lost his balance and hit the ground. Missouri ran over and knelt on the grass beside him. "David?" She shook his shoulders. "Are you okay?"

He opened his eyes and grabbed her wrist. "I'm better than fine." With a lot of effort, he sat up, still holding Missouri's wrist. "You are gorgeous. Give me another kiss."

"David, you are absolutely drunk out of your mind. Go home and sleep it off." Wrenching free of his grip, Missouri jumped to her feet and fled down the gravel path toward the garden exit.

Chapter Eleven

Missouri tossed and turned all night, getting little if any sleep. She couldn't get the picnic with David out of her mind. Had he been teasing her about modeling, trying to get a reaction, or had he been serious? Was he too drunk to even know or remember everything he said? Should she complain to someone about his behavior?

She quickly turned on her computer and "Googled" David Harris artist. It was true. He really was known in the New York area for his nude paintings and he did teach figure drawing and anatomy at Pratt. She read through a long list of awards, juried art shows, gallery exhibitions, artist in residences, summer workshops, teaching positions, etc. His bio was impressive.

What little sleep Missouri had was disturbed by dreams about her and David in which she reclined nude on an overstuffed crimson red chaise with lots of plump black pillows – like a classical painting hanging in the museum. In her dreams, David sat at an easel, sketching her with *conté* crayon. She was dozing in the afternoon sun. Suddenly she was awakened by David, covering her body with kisses. But as she began to unbutton his shirt, his face dissolved into that of Doyle's. She screamed and woke up in her own bed, gasping for breath, her heart racing, her body trembling. She wondered if these dreams were caused by a frustrated libido or too many pathetic letters from her ex?

•   •   •   •   •

Missouri rushed into David's class five minutes late. Fortunately, the model had not arrived. Once the male or female model was disrobed and posed, the studio door was locked and no one was allowed in or out. As she pulled out paper, pens and pencils, she prayed that the model was a girl with lots of smooth curves.

David, who was standing on the other side of the studio with his arms folded across his chest, watched Missouri getting ready to work. When she sat down on her bench, he walked over to her. "So nice that you could join us, Mrs. Rothman." An amused expression plastered his face. "It doesn't look like our model is coming this morning. Would you mind filling in for her?"

Conversations throughout the studio halted. Students turned their attention to David and Missouri, who stood up and glared at him. She could feel her face burning, but it was probably not from embarrassment, but from anger. "No problem, Mr. Harris, but why don't you model first? When you get tired, I'll take your place."

David sucked in his cheeks and pursed his lips. He walked around Missouri, eyeing her thoughtfully, his steps echoing loudly in the hushed studio. Abruptly the classroom door burst open and a flustered young woman ran in, clutching her black satin robe together in front.

"I'm so sorry," she squealed, brushing blonde tousled hair out of her eyes. "My alarm didn't go off. Am I too late?"

"Almost, Ms. Timberlake." David quickly glanced sideways at Missouri. "Mrs. Rothman and I were just getting ready to take your place. Fortunately, you've saved us both the embarrassment."

•   •   •   •   •

Half an hour into class, Missouri was ready to write it off as a complete loss. She couldn't draw anything. And David seemed to be hovering around her more than usual. Come on, Missouri, she screamed to herself. Focus, focus, focus!

"What is your problem today, Mrs. Rothman?" David asked softly from behind her.

Caught off guard, Missouri dropped her charcoal stick, which shattered into half a dozen unsalvageable pieces as it hit the terra cotta floor. "Oh, dang it all!" she yelled in disgust. She'd paid three Euros for it at Zecchi's last week. Now she'd have to buy another one. She was totally pissed.

David grunted and moved on. "Don't forget, everyone, you're expected to turn in your best drawing at the end of class."

Missouri sunk down wearily on her bench. Yeah, right, she thought, glaring at him. Like she was going to have anything worth turning in.

•   •   •   •   •

The class ended, and the model dressed and left. Missouri hurried to finish her only drawing. Her other attempts had ended up in the trash. This final one would have to do. If only the rib cage didn't look so out of line with the backbone and pelvis. She added a stroke, smudged the charcoal with her finger and stepped back. Her breath cut through her front teeth in an audible hiss of self-disgust. She twisted her wrist and checked the time. "Dang!" she muttered under her breath. No more time. It would have to do.

Missouri put away her art supplies and headed toward the door where David stood talking with two other students. She handed him her drawing and turned to leave.

"One moment, Mrs. Rothman. I'd like to speak to you, please," David called after her.

She turned her head in his direction, but did not stop moving toward the door. "Sorry, Mr. Harris, but I'm late for an appointment." She quickly exited the studio and found Gabriella waiting for her. "What are you doing here, Gabby?" she asked, not slowing her pace.

Gabriella moved in step beside her. "What's going on between you and Monsieur Harris?"

"Nothing is going on."

"*Pardonne-moi*, Madame Rothman, but something is going on. First of all, you went to bed *très tût* and kept me awake all night with your moans and groans. Second, you did badly in class today. And finally, you act...mmmmm...how you say...*bourru* we say in French...testy, I think...cantankerous, *oui?*"

Missouri halted in her tracks and faced her roommate. "Me? Testy? Cantankerous?" she yelled. "How dare you call me..." She paused as she saw Gabby's eyes widen. Missouri's shoulders sank. She sighed wearily. "You're right, Gabby, I have my mind on other things. I'm sorry. I apologize for my rude behavior."

The two women continued walking slowly, side by side in silence.

"Can a friend buy you a *caffè latte?*" Gabriella asked.

"Certainly," Missouri said. "I think a *caffè latte* is exactly what I need."

• • • •

"*Zut!*" exclaimed Gabriella when Missouri told her about David asking her to model for him. "*Mais non!* Maybe he was serious, *ma cheri.*"

"I don't think so!"

"But is he not known for his earthy, sensual nude paintings?"

"So is Andrew Wyeth and I wouldn't model nude for him either."

"Most definitely not, *ma cheri*. He died a few years ago. Maybe you model for his son, *oui?*"

"Absolutely not!"

"Why not? Moral reasons or something else?"

"No, no, no! Because I'm TOO old and TOO fat! There's a reason Andrew Wyeth switched from Helga to Siri."

"Tut, tut! Look at Sophia Loren. She must have 30 years on you. Men all over the world still consider her a sex goddess."

"Good, then let her model in the nude for David."

"Aaaaaah. *Je comprends.* How you say, the bottom line here is..."

"Huh?"

"I think the anger and friction between you two is not what it seems. *Non?*"

"I don't understand, Gabby. What are you talking about?"

"You are not annoyed at him because he asked you to model for him. *Non,* you are angry because of something else. *Oui?*"

Missouri sat in silence, running her finger around the top of the coffee cup.

"What, *Cheri?* Did he try to make love with you?" Gabriella asked, reaching out and touching Missouri's arm.

Missouri felt her cheeks begin to burn. She leaned forward and whispered, "No." She hesitated. "He...uh...he kissed me."

"And?"

"And that's it, Gabby. Nothing more."

"A man kisses you and you are upset? You crazy American woman!"

"You don't understand."

"*Oui,* I do not. Explain it to me, *s'il vous plaît.*"

"He grabbed me and kissed me hard and wouldn't let go."

"In France we would say he kissed with passion. Didn't that excite you?"

Missouri's mouth turned up at the corners in spite of herself. "Okay, I'll admit there were some flutterings down under."

Gabriella leaned back giggling. "You silly American woman. If you liked it, you should have kissed him back. It's called *l'amour.* You are unhappy because his passionate kiss aroused you, *oui?*"

Missouri sighed. "No."

"Then what is your *probleme?*"

"I don't know, okay?" Missouri spat out each word staccato. "We shouldn't be kissing like that."

"Why is that?"

"Duh! He's my teacher."

"So?"

"He's a baby, Gabby. I'm 10 years older than he is." Missouri sighed.

"Ten years is nothing, *ma cheri*. In California there are plenty of women dating men 20 years younger than them."

Missouri threw her arms up in the air. "Yes, and the men are either "boy toys" or *gigolos*, and the women are all desperate."

Gabby chewed her lip thoughtfully and spoke softly. "Perhaps the women who turn down the opportunity of loving a younger man are too scared to give it a chance."

Missouri opened and closed her mouth several times, but couldn't verbalize a reply. She wondered if Gabby could be right.

Chapter Twelve

During the days prior to a five-day field trip to Venice, Missouri was polite to David in class. Occasionally, when she glanced up from her work, he would be looking at her from across the room. When he stopped behind her to view her work, the back of her neck would tingle and her heart would beat faster. Even though he didn't try to talk to her during class, after class she made sure she was among the first students out the door. In the evenings, she avoided the *caffè* bar scene and retired to the apartment early. She even wore a rubber band around her wrist and whenever she found herself thinking about him and the afternoon in Boboli Gardens, she would snap the rubber band painfully against her skin.

The day before the class left for Venice, David took them to the Galleria dell'Academy to see Michelangelo's most important works. But the only work that Missouri really cared about was *David*. As far as she was concerned, Michelangelo's other masterpieces – like *Quatro Prigioni* (Four Prisoners) or a statue of *St. Matthew* – were just added extras. She thought she was prepared for seeing Michelangelo's colossal nude at last. After all, had she not seen the famous copies located in front of the Palazzo Vecchio in the Piazza della Signoria and in the middle of Piazzale Michelangelo?

But as soon as Missouri entered the museum and saw *David* towering above everyone at the end of the Hall of Prisoners, she realized she was not prepared at all. As she walked slowly down the hall, she could see a huge crowd of tourists standing at the statue's base, their arms raised high to take cell phone photos.

She made her way to the front of the horde and looked up at *David*, sucking in a deep breath at the sight of him. "You are so beautiful!" she cried out, but she couldn't hear herself above the roar of voices loudly chatting and speaking in many different tongues. "You are absolutely perfect in every way." All 17 feet tall of him standing on his pedestal throne, making him three times the size of a real man. She had known he was tall, but in all the photos he looked much smaller. How could you really tell his actual size until you were standing beside him? She gawked at the size of his toes and her eyes moved up his body. Sure, it was only carved stone, she thought, but the muscles and veins seemed so real. And everything else, too.

Missouri was not sure how long she had been standing in that one spot, her eyes feasting on every inch of this beautiful, perfect man. She was not aware that her class had moved on to study works by other nearby artists. She stood oblivious to everyone and everything, until a voice shouted in her ear.

"Mrs. Rothman! I'm talking to you!"

She jumped and turned so abruptly that she nearly butted heads with a very annoyed human David. "What?" Her face began to burn like she had been caught doing something really bad.

David pointed down the hall to *David's* right, where members of her class were huddled watching the two of them expectantly. "They are waiting on you to finish ogling and gawking over *David's* magnificent body."

"Oh. Sorry." Head bowed, Missouri hurried over to her waiting classmates, who looked quite amused.

• • • • •

At last, the departure day for Venice arrived. Missouri felt relief with a tiny twinge of disappointment when the bus she was on pulled away from the station without David. Obviously, he was on the second bus. Not that he could have sat next to her with Gabriella occupying the aisle seat.

Since no vehicles of any kind were allowed in Venice, the buses were unloaded at a car park on the outskirts of the city. All transportation was done on foot or by boat. Students hefted their back packs and duffle bags and followed Alessandra DeMarco along small canals and over numerous bridges to their hotel, the Pensione Seguso on the Giudecca canal.

"Look," Gabriella said, glancing at the evening schedule. "We're free until dinner."

Missouri fell across the bed and thought how easy it would be to just lie there until 7 o'clock. "What did you want to do, Gabby?"

Gabriella unfolded a piece of notebook paper she'd pulled from her shirt pocket. "Shop, of course. Here *Madame*, I have a list of six designer dress shops. Interested?"

Missouri rolled her eyes. "You gotta be kidding?" As far as Missouri was concerned, a root canal would be more entertaining.

"*Mais non*! This may be my only chance. The rest of the time we'll be touring museums and churches. Sure you don't want to go? *S'il vous plait?*"

"Sorry, Gabby. This is Venice. I want to see it all."

Gabrielle shrugged, grabbed her bag and opened the door. "*Au revoir, Cheri!*"

Missouri smiled and shook her head. It was all about priorities. She smoothed out a map of Venice on the bed and found the closest *vaporetti* stop. Alessandra told her riding the waterbus was just like riding the city bus. *Vaporetti* stops were located along large canals, and the waterbus had different routes.

After purchasing a three-day ticket and checking the waterbus service map carefully, Missouri decided on the #1 route, the *Accelerato*, which was a slow boat that went down the Grand Canal, stopping at every stop.

Camera in hand, Missouri took an outside seat in the bow. It was a perfect day for *vaporetti* joy-riding, she decided – a cloudless blue sky with lots of sun, temperatures in the 70s, a light breeze blowing in from the ocean. As the boat puttered along, Missouri gloried in the sea breeze and salt spray in her face. She marveled over the sights of Venice -- gondolas steered by colorful gondoliers, working boats on the canal and brightly colored old buildings that lined the canals. From her tour guide book, she recognized the Doge's Palace, the Campanile of San Marco, the Zecca, Santa Maria della Salute, the Academy, the Rialto Bridge and San Simeone Piccolo.

The *vaporetta* she was riding continued on its slow course, making stops along the way. People got off and new passengers came aboard, but Missouri was oblivious to everything except the sights and sounds of Venice. Suddenly at one stop, someone came up behind her and started screaming in Italian. She turned in her seat to see a short red-faced man in a red-and-white striped shirt, tendrils of black hair clinging to his sweaty forehead. Leaning over at the waist, he kept throwing his arms and hands out to the sides and screaming, "*Basta! Basta!*"

Dumbfounded at his anger, Missouri jumped to her feet and stared at him. She thought *basta* meant 'stop it,' but stop what? A growing group of rubberneckers on the dock waved their arms around and shouted down at her in Italian. She felt her face burning. She did not know what she had done to make the man so mad.

"He's telling you it's the end of the line. Get off!" The male voice shouted to her from the dock on the other side of the boat. Keeping an eye on the agitated Italian, Missouri passed by him and ran to the boat's exit ramp.

Grabbing an extended hand that appeared from above, Missouri was pulled up onto the dock.

"*Grazie, Signor*," she said, looking up into the face of her benefactor – David Harris. Missouri gasped and pulled her hand away from his grasp. She turned to flee in the opposite direction, but found herself confronted by half a dozen scuzzy-looking waterfront workers who were leering at her with narrow eyes, twisted smiles and wicked expressions. Missouri could only think two words: mob mentality.

"Unfortunately, the end of the line for this route is the commercial wharf area where the cargo ships come in. My suggestion is that you smile and nod and move close to me. Take my hand and we'll walk casually over to the other *vaporetta* stop and catch one going in the opposite direction." David's calming voice reached out to her.

Missouri didn't see any choice but to do as David suggested. A *vaporetta* cruised in as they stepped up to the adjacent dock and onto the boat. As the *vaporetta* pulled away, Missouri sat down on a seat, breathing hard. Tears ran down her cheeks. She held out her trembling hands. "Look, I'm so scared, I'm shaking all over. I don't know what would have happened if you hadn't been there." David reached into his back pocket and handed her a handkerchief. She wiped her eyes. Then her head shot up and she looked directly at David. "Just what were you doing on that dock?" she asked. "Were you following me?"

David sat down next to her. "Hey, what happened to your undying gratitude?"

She locked her eyes on his and waited.

He sighed and rubbed the back of his neck. "If you must know, Mrs. Rothman, you're right. I was following you," he admitted. "Lucky for you."

"You were on the *vaporetta* with me the whole time?"

David nodded.

"You were standing on the dock because you knew it was the end of the line?"

David nodded and smiled. "Hey, at least I was smart enough to get off. I didn't just sit there and wait to be thrown off."

Missouri blinked. "What a crock of possum guts! You can kiss my grits!"

David laughed so hard, he bent over double.

She stared at him intently. It wasn't long before she was laughing with him. Finally she sobered up and wiped her eyes. "Now explain to me why you were following me?"

"What do you think? To apologize."

"For what?"

"I'm not sure. I know you've been upset with me, but I don't know why. I guess I did or said something to make you angry. So I want to apologize for whatever I said or did that made you freeze me out of your life. Please forgive me, and give me a chance to redeem myself." He looked at her imploringly. "Please, Missouri?"

Missouri chewed on her lower lip. It really was a strain on her emotionally to remain upset with him, she thought. She did miss their long talks and his company, too. And didn't he just save her from a screaming mob? "You seriously don't remember what happened?"

David shook his head and sighed. "Only bits and pieces. I know I had too much wine. I know I was so drunk I passed out. I woke up face down in the grass and dirt with a splitting headache and a body covered in ants."

Missouri nodded. "Anything else?"

"Maybe I kissed you?"

"Yes you did."

"I didn't force myself on you, did I? We didn't do anything we might both regret later, did we?" He grimaced. "The last time I ever got rip-roaring drunk was at my bachelor's party, and I didn't remember anything about it the next day either. I swore I would never get that drunk, again."

"You really don't remember anything else?"

David grimaced. "Missouri, please, you're killing me. I can't take not knowing how bad I was. Was I so bad you won't ever forgive me?"

Missouri watched a gondola with an embracing couple float by. A costumed gondolier stood in the stern crooning a love song. She envied the love the couple shared.

"Missouri, this is the stop for your *penzione* – unless you want to ride to the end of the line this way." David rose and helped her to her feet. She followed him off the boat. "Well, are you going to forgive me or not?" he asked, looking at her with his sad blue eyes.

Missouri fought down a smile. "On one condition."

"Anything. You name it. I'll even wear a 'I'm a Dirty Dog' shirt. I'll get down on my hands and knees and push a peanut across the *piazza* with my nose. Do you want me to throw myself at your feet and grovel?" He dropped down to his knees.

"David, stop it! People are staring at us." Missouri glanced at a man and a woman waiting for the next *vaporetta*. She reached down and tried to pull him to his feet, but he wouldn't budge. "Okay, I forgive you. Now get up and stop acting like an idiot."

David stood up, a dopey grin on his face. He grabbed her hand and planted a dozen kisses on it. "Thank you, oh magnificent goddess, for granting me my wish."

"You're embarrassing me. I'm getting annoyed."

David straightened up and wiped the grin off his face. "And my one condition I promise to adhere to?"

"You must never ever drink more than one glass of wine in my presence," she said. Silently to herself, she added another condition that he better not ever mention anything about using her as a nude model.

"Thank you, Mrs. Rothman." He looked at her solemnly and shook her hand. "I'm glad we can be friends, again."

"Back up and wait one minute. I only agreed to forgive you. I don't remember anything about being friends."

David frowned. "What?"

Missouri laughed to herself as she turned and walked toward her *penzione*. She looked back at David. "See you at dinner, *mio amico*."

· · · · · ·

After dinner with the group, Missouri agreed to have coffee with David. From the *caffè* bar, they ambled through *San Marco Square*, past the *Doges Palace* to the Grand Canal where they found an empty bench overlooking *San Giorgio Maggiore* across the water.

Missouri sighed. Venice at night was fascinating, she thought, and romantic. "That church across the canal looks just like a stage set. I should try to capture it in watercolor. Have you ever painted the view from here?"

"Countless times," he said. "So did Modigliani. He loved Venice."

"What is the name of that church?"

"*San Giorgio Maggiore*," he said. "The church and the monastery were built mid-16th century. If you visit the church, you'll find two late Tintorettos on the chancel walls, *The Last Supper* and *Gathering of the Manna*."

Missouri nodded and looked down the canal. "The lighting on these wonderful old buildings is just glorious."

"Yes, Venice is beautiful, but like any city anywhere, it has its problems."

"Are you referring to the flooding problems and stories of the city sinking into the sea?"

"Flooding is a major problem. Smaller annoying ones include garbage, rats, mosquitos, the summer-time stench, water pollution, too many tourists and a burgeoning population."

"Remind me not to hire you to promote and market Venice to the travel industry."

David reached out and covered her right hand with his left. "May I have permission to hold your hand."

"Looks like you already are."

They both laughed. David stood and pulled Missouri to her feet. "I have a room with a balcony that overlooks the Grand Canal. Have you forgiven me enough to check out the view and share some *chianti* I bought this afternoon?"

Missouri could not see his face in the dim lighting along the canal, but his voice sounded sincere. She was feeling very comfortable with him and enjoying his company. During their evening walk, he had talked to her some more about his favorite Italian artist Modigliani and other artists who lived and worked in Paris during, before and after World War I. She wanted to learn more about their lives, their art, their haunts and the women they painted.

What the heck, Missouri, she told herself. You're attracted to him. He's charming. You love his company. Why can't you just enjoy the moment? "All right, David," she finally answered. "Let's go to your room and check out your great view." But I'm going to be cautious, David Harris. You're absolutely not painting me naked.

•　　•　　•　　•　　•

David had not exaggerated about his balcony. The view of the Grand Canal was in Missouri's opinion totally magical. She and David stood at the marble rail, sipped *chianti* and watched the boat traffic on the Canal. Gondoliers guided passengers to destinations throughout the city. Occasionally, songs of *amoré* sung by the gondoliers wafted up to their balcony. David was quick to point out ambulance, fire and police boats. Private yachts for hire cruised the Canal, as did business-owned boats that delivered goods to businesses and restaurants. This included everything from fruits and vegetables to office furniture and construction equipment. When she closed her eyes, Missouri could smell the ocean, intermingled with diesel fumes from the *vaporetti* and other boats.

A contented Missouri sighed happily. "I could stand here all day and never get bored."

David put his left arm around her shoulders and pulled her close. His hand slipped to the back of her neck, where his fingers began a gentle massage. With his right hand, he tilted her face up to his. "You are one amazing woman, Missouri. You're sensitive, kind, witty, charming, creative, attractive and a talented artist. Please stop me if any of this offends you."

"Not yet, but keep going."

Gently he touched her lips with his own and kissed her ever so tenderly. This time she did not pull away. No alarm bells went off in her head. Just tingly feelings in her abdomen. She smiled at him. "You have a way with words, David. I like that. Tell me more."

He gathered her tightly into his arms. She could feel the warmth of his body pressed against hers. The kiss that followed robbed her of her breath. "Wow," she said, coming up for air. "You're a pretty good kisser for a youngster."

"If it won't offend you, I'd like to take you inside and show you what a youngster like me can really do." He pulled back and looked directly into her eyes. His voice took on a serious edge. "But I don't want you to do anything you feel uncomfortable with. And especially not anything that will get you upset with me, again. That's why I'm only drinking one glass of wine."

Missouri backed David off the balcony into the room. "There's one thing you should know about us older women, David." She began unbuttoning his shirt and pushing him backwards onto the bed. "Once we make up our minds to do something, there's no turning back."

Chapter Thirteen

Humming the melody of "Some Enchanted Evening," Missouri lugged two bags of groceries up the stairs to the apartment in Florence. Gabriella promised to cook dinner if Missouri stopped by the Prego food store for the prosciutto, fruit, bread, cheese, pasta and olives. As she hummed, Missouri thought of the intimacies she had shared with David during their time in Venice. She dared not think about the long-term prospect of their relationship. She only wanted to think about the happiness their relationship brought with the moment.

Smiling happily, she knocked on the door for Gabriella so she wouldn't have to put down the groceries to retrieve her key. "Gabby, open the door. It's the grocery delivery lady." She was still humming happily when the massive metal door opened, and she found herself nose to nose with her ex-husband Doyle. "Some Enchanted Evening" ended in mid-note as her gaping speechless mouth tried to force her brain to respond. "What are you doing here?"

Doyle stepped aside to avoid a potentially serious testicle injury from one of the shopping bags. "Hello to you, too, Missouri. Is that the best response you can come up with for a man who took a leave of absence to fly across the Atlantic to visit his wife?"

"Ex-wife," Missouri corrected him as she headed toward the kitchen, passing an apologetic Gabby.

"*Pardonne-moi,*" Gabriella whispered, taking the bags from Missouri. "I am sorry. He said he needed to see you. He was groveling, Missouri. I can't stand to see a man grovel."

Missouri touched Gabriella's shoulder, "It's okay, Gabby. You take care of the groceries and I'll take care of Doyle." Gabriella went into the kitchen and shut the door behind her. Missouri turned around to face Doyle. She could feel her breathing and heartbeat increasing and her cheeks beginning to burn. "Okay, Doyle, what do you want?"

Doyle took a step in her direction, his hands and arms reaching out for her.

Missouri did a quick sidestep over to the sofa and sat down. She indicated a small upholstered chair across from her.

Doyle inhaled and exhaled loudly, and sat down. "How are you doing, Missouri?"

Ahh, thought Missouri. She could almost hear the wheels turning and the gears shifting in his brain as he tried to say the right thing. "Everything was going great until two minutes ago. Now why don't you tell me why you're here."

Doyle cleared his throat. "I came over with our sons for a Tuscan vacation."

Missouri's breath hissed out. She could not believe that Michael and Cody were in Florence with their dad. She was happy at the thought of seeing her sons, but apprehensive about why they had come. "I see. So while you were in the neighborhood, you thought you'd just drop in to see me?"

"That's exactly right," he said, nodding his head.

"Hogwash!" She jumped to her feet. "I don't believe that. You thought that if you confronted me in person, I couldn't ignore you like I do your letters and email."

Doyle jumped to his feet. "Haven't you?"

"Haven't I what?"

He threw his arms in the air. "Ignored my letters?"

Missouri did not respond.

"Did you even read them?" he asked, scowling.

She lifted her chin. "Maybe one or two. I'm too busy to fool with any form of mail."

"But you have plenty of time to write Michael and Cody and your friends."

"Yes, I do have priorities. One of those is that I don't have to respond to an ex-husband who left me for a younger woman."

"We have two sons. We were married 32 years. We have connections. Would it kill you to answer my letters?"

She looked him right in the eye. "Doyle, you divorced me for Miss Perky Boobs. I owe you nothing. I don't remember reading anything in the divorce papers about having to read your letters or respond to them."

A dark red flush of anger spread up Doyle's neck and covered his face. "We have history, Missouri. Are you going to piss on that and throw it away?"

"Funny thing none of that meant anything to you last year."

Doyle huffed. "The divorce was a mistake, Missouri. I see that now. One that I regret very much. I was wrong. I was a complete idiot. I'm sorry, okay? How much longer are you going to punish me for one little indiscretion and mid-life crisis?"

Missouri turned away from Doyle. She wasn't sure how much more of this she could take. "Where are Michael and Cody?"

"At our hotel. I thought the four of us could go out to dinner together. You know, like a family...like the old days."

"Yes, I would definitely like to see my sons." Missouri turned to face Doyle. "How long will you be in Florence?"

"As long as it takes." Doyle took another step closer to her.

"As long as it takes to do what?" she asked, not sure if she wanted to hear the answer.

"As long as it takes to get you to forgive me and to convince you that I still love you."

"Life is short, Doyle. I forgive you for all the pain you caused me. And I believe that in some way, you really do love me." Doyle closed the gap between them and tried to hug her, but Missouri pushed him away. "Don't do that."

Doyle took a step back. "I don't understand your problem, Missouri. I told you I love you. "You're the best thing that ever happened to me. I want you home with me and our sons. I want to marry you and spend the rest of my life with you. I want us to grow old together. I believe that's what you want, too."

"Dammit, Doyle..." Missouri could feel her stomach knotting up. "I don't have time to debate this with you. I have homework to do." She didn't understand why Doyle had to come to Italy now and try to stir up old feelings. She had put him and her marriage behind her. She had moved on. Why couldn't he do the same?

"What about dinner tonight?"

"No, I'm not ready for a foursome dinner, Doyle, but I want to see Michael and Cody. Would you please ask them to meet me at Ivan's *caffe* bar around 8 o'clock tonight?"

"Just the boys, not me?"

He sounded pathetic to Missouri, but she wasn't going to give in. "Only Michael and Cody." She wanted them to meet David. She wanted them to see how happy she was studying and living in Florence. She wanted them to understand why she wasn't ready to hop a plane back to Georgia.

• • • • •

Missouri, Gabriella and David were on their second *cappucino* when Michael and Cody walked into the bar. Missouri rose from her seat and hurried over to hug her sons.

"Whoa, Mom! You look really hot!" Cody said, looking her up and down. "You've lost more weight, too. This Tuscan lifestyle must agree with you."

Michael stood straight and tall like the career military officer he was. "Cody's right, Mom. You do look good. Cody said you'd lost a lot of weight and shaped up, but you look much better than I thought you would. You are one hell of a beautiful woman."

"Thanks, guys. That's a real boost for my self-esteem." With her arms around their waists, she walked them over to the table. "Gabriella, I want you to meet my sons, Michael and Cody." Gabriella stood up and shook their hands.

"*Enchante*, Michael...Cody...I am happy to make your acquaintance. I have heard *magnifique* things about both of you. Mmmmmm, such gorgeous hunks!" She kissed her fingertips.

"Gabby, that's enough. Much more and their heads will expand in size." Missouri turned back to her grinning sons. "Michael, Cody...meet my favorite professor and good friend David Harris." Cody and Michael shook David's hand and sat down with Missouri.

Gabriella remained standing and excused herself. "*Pardone moi*," she said, "but I have several chapters of art history to read before tomorrow. Have a good evening."

"Was that your roommate, Mom?" asked Cody, as he watched Gabby leave the *caffe* bar.

"Yes, she keeps me out of trouble and well-fed. She's a great cook!"

"What about me? Aren't I a great cook, too?" David reached out and covered Missouri's hand with his own.

Cody raised his eyebrows in surprise. Michael's eyes narrowed. Missouri blushed. "Yes, David, you're a good cook, too." She quickly pulled her hand back from David and placed it in her lap, but she knew it was too late. Her sons were not stupid.

"Now that we have that settled," David said, turning to Cody and Michael, "Is this your first trip to Italy?"

"Yes," they both answered at once.

"What have you seen so far?" David asked.

"Our hotel room," Michael said.

"That funny bridge that looks like it's covered with condos," added Cody.

"The Ponte Vecchio?" David asked.

"Yeah, that's what they call it. And the gigantic green and white church with the awesome orange dome," continued Cody.

"The Duomo," said David with a smile. "You've barely scratched the surface of what there is to see in Florence."

"We didn't come to Florence to see the sights," butted in Michael. "We came to see Mom."

David looked at Missouri and smiled. "I like that. They didn't come to Florence to see great works of art. They came to see you. Doesn't that make you feel really special?"

Missouri looked at her sons. "Yes, that gives me a warm, fuzzy feeling." She smiled and stood up. "I love you both very much." She kissed each one on the cheek. "I'm getting me a cup of hot chocolate. Can I get anyone else something?"

"Yes, hot chocolate, please, with whipped cream...con panne, right?" Cody said.

Missouri laughed. "Yes, con panne."

As soon as Missouri was out of ear shot, Michael turned to David abruptly and asked, "Are you sleeping with our mother?"

Cody emitted a strangled sound. "Michael, that's none of your business," Cody said, but he turned to David to see if he would answer the question.

David leaned back in his chair and crossed his arms over his chest. He smiled and eyed Michael with a look of amusement on his face. "Why do you want to know? What's it to you?"

"She's our mother, that's why," Michael said angrily. "If you're having a sexual relationship with her, then we need to know."

"Why is that?" David asked, still smiling.

Michel and Cody exchanged glances. Cody shrugged. Michael scowled and popped his neck. "We can't have her having an affair behind Dad's back," an agitated Michael said.

David shook his head and continued to smile. "Correct me if I'm wrong, but aren't your parents divorced because your father was having an affair with a younger woman."

"That's none of your business," yelled Michael, rising so abruptly from his chair that it fell over.

David stood and pointed a finger at Michael. "Yes, that's exactly my point. Your mother is a beautiful, talented, exciting and single woman. What she does in private is none of your business."

"Hey! What's going on here?" asked Missouri, returning to the table with two steaming mugs. "I could hear you from the other side of the bar." She looked at Cody, who was staring intently at his feet, and then to a red-faced Michael, who picked up his overturned chair and sat down.

"Nothing's going on," David said. "I was just telling your sons that I need to head back to the studio to do some work. I'm sure they would like some private special time with their mom. Right guys?"

Cody and Michael mumbled something.

David bussed Missouri's cheeks, Italian-style. "Good night, Cody. Michael." He shook their hands in turn. "If I don't see you, again, have a safe flight home."

Concerned and puzzled, Missouri watched David walk out the door. When she looked down at Cody and Michael, they both gazed at their hands and refused to look her in the eye. She sat down slowly. "Okay, fellows, who wants to tell me what went down while I was gone?"

Neither responded. "Cody?" Missouri touched her youngest son on his forearm. "I'm waiting."

Cody glanced at his mother briefly. "I'm not sure. Something between Michael and David."

Missouri turned to her oldest son. "Michael?"

Michael shot his brother a nasty look. He shifted his jaw and squirmed in his seat. After a few seconds of silence, he looked steadily at Missouri and took a deep breath. "Okay, Mom, it's like this. We don't like him."

Missouri closed her eyes for a few seconds and steeled herself. "I don't care if you like him or not, Michael. He's my professor and my friend."

"Mom, I don't think he can be trusted."

"Why do you say that?"

"Do I have to spell it out for you? The man is an art professor for Pete's sake. Everyone knows all they do is paint their female students in the nude and take them to bed. If you think he honestly cares about you, then you're being naïve."

Missouri looked at her fuming son. He was so much like his father – quick to judge and always right. "Michael, I see what's going on here. This has nothing to do with David's merits. You see him as someone who stands between me and your dad. I could be dating Brad Pitt or the CEO of Sony or a U.S. senator and you wouldn't like them either. Right?"

"Yeah, Mom, you're absolutely right," Michael blurted out. "Your place is with Dad."

"Thank you for being honest. Now you two listen to me: This is my life and I'll do with it whatever I want. I gave your father the best years of my life and he dumped me for some young twit. I'm going to live my new life as a single woman the way I want to live it."

"But what about Dad?" Cody asked. "He told you he was sorry. He just wants you to give him another chance."

"Yeah, Mom, what about what Dad wants?" Michael asked, standing up. "He's groveled, he's apologized and he's begged you to forgive him. He flew all the way here to take you back to Georgia. What more does he have to do?"

"You two just don't understand. I'm not the same person I was when your father left me over a year ago. Can you see that? Haven't you noticed?"

Michael shifted weight from one leg to the other and glanced furtively at Cody. "Yeah, Mom, I see that you've changed," Michael admitted begrudgingly.

Cody nodded eagerly. "Oh, yeah, Mom, you're a 'hot fox' now." He grinned and scrunched his nose.

Missouri felt a little warmth on her cheeks. She wondered if it was embarrassment or a hot flash. "'Hot fox' is not what I'm aiming for. I'm becoming a stronger person, and I know what I want to be when I grow up."

"But Mom," protested Michael, "Dad said you can still be an artist when you come home."

"Yeah, Mom," Cody stood up next to his brother, "you could paint and draw and enter juried art shows and sell your stuff in the galleries."

"And I'll make you a Web site with links to all the art organizations in town," offered Michael, in his efforts to appease his mother. "Sandy Cooper's grandmother sells her homemade soaps that way."

"Will everyone please calm down. As soon as I return to Athens, I plan to set up a studio. And thank you, Michael, a Web site to show off my work would be well appreciated."

Michael heaved a sigh of relief. "Well, thank goodness you're coming to your senses."

Cody ran over to his mother and hugged her. "Mom, I'm so glad. Let's call Dad so he can get you a seat on the plane with us."

"But..." she said loudly to get their attention, "I'm not going home yet. I have another year of study here."

"What?" Cody piped up. "Dad might not be willing to wait a year for you to come home."

"Michael, Cody, listen to me carefully. I gave up my life, my dreams and a college scholarship to marry your father. But I have no regrets because I was able to travel and raise two wonderful sons. However, now I have an opportunity to fulfill my own dreams."

"Couldn't you finish your dreams in Athens?" Cody asked.

"My dream is here in Florence. My dream is to finish my studies here. This is my top priority. I am not leaving Italy until my program of study is over."

"No, Mom, you're not staying here. Listen to me," Michael said sharply, sounding exactly like his father. "You're leaving with us. Dad loves you and he wants to reunite this family. But his patience is running out. If this art program is more important to you than us as a family, then you are selfish, unreasonable and unappreciative."

Missouri leaned her face towards Michael's until their noses were only inches apart. She could feel the fury of her anger surging throughout her body. "There is no family to reunite. You and Cody are gone. Your father divorced me and left, too. You can call me selfish, unreasonable and unappreciative, but I'm not leaving Italy until I've finished the art program. If your father can't deal with that, that's his problem." Then she straightened herself up as tall as she could. "Thank you for coming to Italy to visit me. Have a nice flight home." She turned on her heel and left the coffee bar without looking back.

Chapter Fourteen

David Harris was swigging down the last drop of strong Italian coffee when the entrance bell sounded. He opened his front window and looked down to the street below to see who was ringing his buzzer. Missouri's sons stood outside the entrance gate. "Damn," he muttered under his breath. He watched as Michael peered through the gate, while Cody stood with his hands in his pockets, his eyes on the cobblestones. David considered pretending he wasn't there, but if they didn't leave, he'd be a hostage in his own apartment and late for class.

Annoyed, David pressed the buzzer to unlock the gate so Michael and Cody could enter the building. He opened his door and watched them trudge up the 500-year-old steps. "Well, you two are up early." He gestured for them to enter his apartment. "I'm surprised to see you. Were you sightseeing nearby? I didn't even know you knew where I lived."

"We didn't," said Michael. "We dropped by the school office, and they directed us here."

That was kind of them, David thought. "Please, sit down, but I do need to leave fairly soon or I'll be late for class."

Michael and Cody sat together on David's dark brown sofa, while he sat opposite them in a well-worn armchair. "Cody and I want to talk to you some more about our mother."

"What about her?"

"Our dad is an idiot," Michael began. "Last year he completely lost his mind and made a fool of himself with this other woman."

"A very, very young woman," added Cody, rolling his eyes. "Now he realizes his mistake and he regrets what he did, right?"

Michael nodded. "Mom tried to get Dad to go to counseling before the divorce, but he refused. Now he's willing to do it. We want Mom to go home and work with Dad to get back together. We want to be a family, again."

David frowned. "Why are you telling me this?"

"Mr. Harris," Cody paused and swallowed, "our parents were married 32 years. We know they still love each other, but your relationship with Mom is complicating a situation that is already complicated. Any feelings Mom has for you are nothing compared to all the years she spent with Dad."

"This is just a summer fling for you," Michael said.

David leaned forward. "What did you say?"

"Sir, we understand how it is." Michael said. "You sweep a female student off her feet and have an exciting romantic time. But once the academic year ends, the students leave, the romance is over. Explain this to Mom. Then she'll be free to go home with Dad and work through their problems. If you've ever had any real feelings for her, you'll walk away."

David jumped to his feet with such force, Michael and Cody sunk back into their seats. "You should leave now." He snatched open the door. "You've said what you came to say. Now go."

Michael and Cody got to their feet and walked slowly out the door. At the top of the staircase, Cody turned and spoke softly to David. "It's true what they say, you know. If you love someone, you have to set them free. If she loves you, she'll come back to you." He followed his brother down the steps.

David slammed the door behind them and slammed his fist into the wall. Immediately, he regretted it. He massaged his hand gently and chided himself for losing his temper. He could not believe that Doyle had sent his sons to try and reason with him. To guilt him into walking away from Missouri. Had the ploy worked? He banged his forehead against the door in frustration.

· · · · ·

David was late getting to class, and Missouri noticed he seemed distracted. But since today was the last day to work on her still-life project, she was too busy to worry about him. She had to concentrate on perfecting her graphite drawing of a violin and bow, sheet music, music stand and bowl of assorted fruit. The few times David wandered by her work space, he left quickly and without comment.

Missouri was the last student to turn in her work. She looked at David questioningly. "Are you okay?"

"Why do you ask?" He added her work to the rest and placed all of them into his large folio carrying case.

"You don't seem yourself."

"How's that?"

"Stressed, I guess. Are you?" She placed her hand on his arm.

"No, maybe just tired." He closed up the case and pulled it off the desk by its handle. "Look, if you're going to be home later this afternoon, I need to drop something off and give you a critique of your work. Can you spare a few minutes?"

"For you, I'll spare the rest of my day and evening." She smiled at him.

Without looking at her, he said, "Good. I'll be there around 5 o'clock. See you then."

Missouri watched him hurry out of the studio. Something was wrong. Something was terribly wrong.

• • • • •

David stood up and examined how his shoes looked on the aged burnt sienna tile. "Look, I need to get back to my studio."

"But you've only been here a few minutes," protested Missouri, who told Gabby to go to dinner without her. She expected David to be there for several hours.

"I only dropped by to return your watercolors and give you a final critique of your work." He looked up briefly and spoke seriously to her. "Missouri, you have a lot of talent. I hope you won't let it go to waste." He moved toward the door.

Missouri followed, placing her hand on his arm in an attempt to halt his hasty retreat. "David, please, can't you stay a little bit longer. I made a pot of coffee."

David shrugged free of her hand. "No, I'm afraid not." He sighed. "I'm sorry, but I really need to go." He took another step toward the door.

"You aren't leaving me without a hug, are you?" she asked poignantly.

David paused in mid-stride and sighed, again. He turned slowly, the eye contact brief. "Sure, one hug for the road."

At first, it was a quick perfunctory embrace on David's part, but when he tried to pull away, Missouri held him tight. The warmth of his body penetrated through her clothes, the smell of his aftershave intoxicated her. She thought she felt him tremble as he tried again to break away. She reached up and gently kissed his lips, but he didn't respond. It was like kissing a total stranger. In shock, she gasped and released her arms from around him. He stepped back, breathing heavily, his face flushed.

Their eyes locked for a second, but he quickly looked away. "I really have to go," he said gruffly.

"David, what's wrong?" She didn't understand. Was this the same man who had wooed her and romanced her? Was Michael right about him? But how could she have been so wrong?

"Nothing's wrong," he replied uneasily. "I can't stay. I need to leave."

Missouri grabbed his arm, but he pulled free. "No, David. Something's going on here. I don't understand. Have I done or said anything to upset you?" Missouri reached out toward him, but he backed up, avoiding her touch.

He looked down at his briefcase and shook his head. "No, it's nothing like that."

"Then what is it? I thought things were going well between us. In Venice, you were warm, responsive and affectionate. Now you seem so cold and mean!"

David's head jerked upwards. His blue eyes stared into hers. "Mean? Because I need to go, I'm mean?"

Missouri's eyes widened and she stepped back. "After our time together in Venice, I thought we had something special between us. David, I really like you. I thought the feeling was mutual."

David closed his eyes and shook his head. "I don't know what you're thinking, Missouri, but there's nothing between us," he said softly, looking at the doorway. "I hope I haven't misled you. I'm just a boring professor who lives only for his art. You're a beautiful woman with a great future and a family that loves you. And even if you do decide to remain in Florence for another year, I won't be teaching any of your classes."

Missouri's head began to spin. She sucked in her breath. "What do you mean? Why not?" Missouri's voice rose, her eyes stung as they filled with tears.

David's fists clenched and unclenched. "Because, dammit, I won't be teaching your class." He swallowed hard. "What was between us is over, don't you get it? It was wrong of me to have you come up to my room in Venice. It was wrong of me to use my status as your professor to take advantage of you."

Missouri grabbed her head and leaned against the wall for support. "You mean it was some sort of sexual fantasy for you to get it on with an older woman? I never meant anything to you? What are you, some sort of sexual predator?" Overtaken with the feelings of a woman scorned, tears of hurt and anger flowing down her cheeks, Missouri reached over started pummeling a shocked David on the chest and shoulders with her fists. "Go on, get out of my sight," she screamed. "Leave now, dammit!" She sobbed loudly and uncontrollably as he left, stumbling in the doorway. "I hate you," she cried out and slammed the door behind him.

Chapter Fifteen

In her worn black vinyl painter's bag, Missouri packed up her watercolors, brushes, paper, water bottle, towel, coffee thermos and cheese panini, and tossed it over her shoulder. She grabbed her Bulldog ball cap and folding camp stool, as she headed out of the apartment. Hurt and confused, Missouri trudged across the river to Via Pellicceria to hire an official taxi.

Through Florence morning rush hour traffic, the taxi driver drove his car slowly through the narrow congested streets until he reached the Ponte Santa Trinita and crossed the Arno. As he headed across the river, away from the center of Florence, the traffic became lighter and the driver attempted unsuccessfully to engage Missouri in conversation. But Missouri's mind was elsewhere. She had not felt this discouraged and hopeless since the day Doyle dropped his divorce bomb on her. Just when she thought she had discovered real happiness, again, the new life she'd worked for – the lemonade she'd carefully made from her lemons – had turned sour.

"*Signora,*" the taxi driver's anxious voice jarred her to reality. "*Signora, ecco,* we are here."

Numbly, Missouri handed over Euros to the driver and forced herself out of the taxi at the Piazza Michelangelo. She looked up at the copy of Michelangelo's *David*, which dominated the busy piazza. Already the parking lot was filling with tourists, motorcoaches, souvenir vendors and artists painting the magnificent vista below. Her favorite spot since the first day David brought the class here, Missouri thought seeing the view and trying to paint it might get her out of her funk. She walked over to the wall that ran along the edge of the overlook and gazed down at the river Arno, its seven bridges and the best view of Florence. Tears rolled down her cheeks as she took in the sight below.

She wiped away the tears and busied herself, first by setting up her stool, then pulling out her painting supplies and getting down to work. Even as she did a quick pencil sketch of the Domo and the river, her mind was on David. She kept replaying last night's unsettling meeting and conversation. How could

I have been so wrong, she wondered, as she squeezed dabs of cadmium red, cobalt blue and cadmium yellow on her white, plastic palette.

Had he decided their age difference really did matter? She started brushing in a bright blue sky and leaving unpainted areas for the white wispy clouds. But no, she argued with herself, that couldn't be it. She had been the only one from the very beginning who had any hang ups over the age issue. It was David who convinced her that age difference didn't matter.

Working with burnt sienna and yellow ochre, Missouri began to bring out the buildings that surrounded the Duomo. Two older women tourists paused behind her to watch her work. Ordinarily, this would have annoyed her and made her self-conscious. But today Missouri didn't notice. As she continued to brush on the watercolor, she could feel her body relaxing into almost a meditative state. By the time she stroked in the brilliantly colored orange tiles of the Duomo and signed her name, she not only sold her panoramic watercolor to one of the tourists for 40 Euros, she also had started forming a plan of action in her mind.

Pulling out a new piece of Fabriano Uno, 130 pounds, cold pressed, Missouri sketched out the medieval gate of Saint Nicolas with the river and city in the background. Even if David was out of her life, she knew she was not going home to Athens, Georgia, like a dutiful child. She was not giving up her newly found independence to return to that old life of groveling, wifely servitude. She found it hard to believe that over a year ago, she would have done anything not to lose her old life as Mrs. Doyle Rothman. But now she knew she had to get out of Florence. She couldn't take a chance on seeing David. She needed a safe place, where she could protect the life of the new Missouri Campbell Rothman.

"Mom, you're here." Missouri, startled, turned to see her son Cody walk up behind her. He gave her a big hug and sat down on the pavement beside her stool, folding up his long legs and crossing his ankles. "Gabriella said you liked to come up here early in the morning and work."

Missouri looked back at her painting. "Yes, I also come here to be alone with my thoughts. It helps the creative process."

Cody looked up wistfully at his mother. "Are you thinking about going home with me and Michael and Dad?"

The left side of Missouri's mouth twitched. She wet the section on her Fabriano Uno paper where the river snaked across. She did not answer Cody's question.

"You're not coming with us, are you?" Cody reached up and touched her arm.

Missouri dropped cerulean blue, gamboge and burnt umber pigment onto the damp paper and watched with satisfaction as her brush pushed and swirled the colors into a painted river. "No, Cody, I'm not." She rinsed her brush in the water. "I plan to remain in Italy and finish what I came here to do."

Cody nodded and turned toward the Florence panorama. "It's really beautiful up here, Mom. I understand why you like to come here."

Missouri continued brushing in color. An uneasy silence prevailed for several minutes. From the corner of her eye, Missouri watched Cody's pensive face. Furrows appeared between his eyes. He nibbled on his lower lip. She knew he was mulling something over in his mind and would open his mouth and speak soon.

Cody finally looked back up at Missouri. "You know, I told Dad and Michael that it wouldn't work. I knew once you made up your mind, there wasn't anything they could do to change it."

"Then why did you come?"

"Just in case I was wrong. Besides, I wanted to be supportive. Dad really wants you back, and I didn't want him to think I was against any reconciliation."

Missouri washed off her brush and placed it on a small rag to dry. She looked at Cody speculatively. "You regret coming over here?"

Cody pulled himself to his feet. "Definitely not," he said emphatically. He waved his arms towards Florence. "I wouldn't have missed seeing this for anything. Besides, Dad picked up the tab. I could never afford this trip on my salary. You know that."

Missouri laughed and stood up to hug her son. "That's my Cody. You didn't come here to drag me back to Georgia against my will. You came along for a good time at your father's expense."

Cody rolled his eyes and examined his Timberland hiking shoes, blushing slightly. "Well, I wanted to see you, too, Mom. Make sure you were doing okay." A breeze rolled uphill from the river and blew Cody's hair.

Missouri brushed Cody's hair off his forehead with her fingers. "I'm happy to see you, too, Cody." She smiled lovingly at her younger son. "I only wish you and Michael had left your dad in Georgia."

Cody helped his mother pack up. They were able to catch a taxi unloading tourists and headed back to Florence, where they were deposited near the

Duomo. Carrying his mother's bag and stool, they walked up Via dei Calzaiuoli towards the river. They paused in front of the Disney Store to admire the American icon Mickey Mouse standing in the store window. When Cody moved across the street to drool over 48 flavors of *gelato*, Missouri urged him into the *trattoria* next door for a large bowl of *ribollita*, a thickened soup made of cabbage, herbs, beans and vegetables, served with large slabs of Tuscan bread.

Cody wiped the soup bowl clean with his last piece of bread. He leaned back in his chair and sighed. "That was better than any soup I've ever tasted. I love the Italian food. Do you think it's possible to buy a traditional Italian cook book here – that's written in English?"

Missouri smiled at her son. She thought she felt her heart swell with the love she had for him. "I found a bookstore near my apartment that carries English versions. And..." She pulled a folded slip of paper out of her sketch book and handed it to him. "Here is the title of a cookbook highly recommended by Alessandra."

· · · · ·

The cookbook section was easy to find by looking for books covered with food. In less than a minute, Missouri tugged *The Delights of Good Italian Cooking* off the shelf. "You'll really like this one, Cody. Lots and lots of full-color photos on every page and all in English."

Cody carried the book to the cashier and pulled out his wallet. "I'm cooking *Crostini di Funghi* and *Risotto ai Asparagi* for dinner."

Missouri gave Cody a one-arm hug. "*Mercato* here we come."

· · · · ·

Missouri sat at the small kitchen table, watching Cody chop up fresh tomatoes and mushrooms. She felt content and happy and bursting with love for her son. Then the moment passed as quickly as it came.

"Mom, are you okay?" Cody asked, measuring out rice to be rinsed.

"Why do you ask?"

"All of a sudden you look very sad. Should we invite David to join us for dinner? Will that make you happy?"

Missouri wandered over to the window that overlooked the busy shopping street below. "David wants nothing to do with me. I don't understand what happened. I thought..." Missouri turned and looked at Cody. "Your father didn't threaten him, did he?"

Cody dumped the rinsed rice in the pot. "No, not Dad."

Missouri stuck her face in Cody's. "If not Dad, then who?"

Cody gulped.

"What did you and Michael do, Cody? Did you go to David's apartment?"

"Maybe."

"Cody! Tell me!" Missouri grabbed his arm. She could not believe that her sons would do that.

Cody wiped his hands on a towel. "Mom, it was nothing. We visited him. We told him that Dad wanted to work things out and that he should back off. That was it."

Holding her head, Missouri backed up to a kitchen chair and collapsed. Cody kept talking, but she couldn't comprehend what he was saying. Her mind was whirling. She could not believe that David cared so little for her that as soon as Michael and Cody told him to back off, he agreed to do so. That was it. She was not taking summer classes at the Academy as she had planned. No way. She had to get away from Florence, but she absolutely wasn't going home with Doyle.

Chapter Sixteen

Missouri's former high school art teacher, Thelma Coley, answered the phone on the first ring. At the sound of her former teacher's voice, Missouri's eyes filled with tears, and she wished she were sitting in the Coleys' living room sipping tea. She knew part of the reason she felt like she did was due to homesickness. The rest was because of David's rejection.

Thelma listened quietly as Missouri poured out her story of woe. "I'm at my wit's end, Thelma. I don't want to go back home with Doyle and my sons. I want to finish my studies here, but I need to get away from David. I need to think and sort things out."

"Yes, dearie, you certainly do. I think I have the perfect solution, but I need to make one phone call first. Could I call you back this evening?"

Missouri wiped her eyes with a tissue. "Yes, please. It will be great if you can help me."

• • • • •

When Missouri's cell phone rang a little after 8 o'clock, Gabriella had just left the apartment to join some of the other students at the coffee bar. "Missouri, this is Thelma."

"Yes? Do you have good news for me?"

"Yes, dearie, I certainly do. Arthur is teaching this summer at the university's Study Abroad Program in Cortona."

Missouri sat down and loosened her death grip on the cell phone. "Yes, I heard about the program from Ron. I looked into it, but Ron said the two-year program in Florence was a better choice for me."

"I agree with Ron on that 100 percent. However, if you need to get a break from Florence – and David – then Arthur is offering you a six-week artist-in-residence position with the Cortona program teaching a special workshop in portraiture."

Relief flooded Missouri's body from head to toes. She sighed loudly. "Oh thank you, thank you, thank you."

"You can thank Arthur. If he didn't think you were talented, he wouldn't be making you this offer. Of course, at the end of six weeks, you must either return to the program in Florence or come back to Georgia."

Missouri sank back into the sofa. "I think six weeks is enough time for me to get my head on straight."

. . . . .

"*Mon Dieu! Oh la vache!* You crazy American woman!" Gabriella banged the heels of her hands into her forehead. "*Incroyable!* Now is not the time to run away. Stay and fight for *l'amour!*"

Missouri dropped her duffle bag by the door. "I can't stay, Gabby. I am suffocating here. I need to get far away from everyone, so I can think."

Gabriella sighed loudly. "*Je ne comprends pas.* Why can't you think here?"

"Because I am being pulled apart by too many forces. Because if I stay in Florence and see David – even from a distance – I will become a crazy American woman." Missouri opened the front door.

Gabriella grabbed Missouri's arm. "What if your family or David ask me where you are?"

Missouri gave her friend a hug. "You will tell no one. I do not want to talk to anyone until I've had time to decide what I want. What is important to me."

"You make big mistake. I feel it here in my heart." She touched her chest. "*Ici. Mon coeur.*"

"I promise I will call you." Missouri picked up her bag. "I must hurry or I will miss my train." She shut the door behind herself as she left.

Three steps down and Missouri heard a muffled "*Merde!*" coming from behind the closed apartment door.

Chapter Seventeen

According to her Italy guide book, Missouri read that Cortona was one of the oldest hill towns in Tuscany. The small walled city, founded by the Etruscans, was a major power during the Middle Ages. Today tourists flocked there because it was scenic, peaceful and quaint with lots of narrow cobblestone alleyways and medieval buildings. Missouri closed her book and gazed out the train window, where the Tuscan countryside zipped by. Yes, she thought, Cortona, sounds like the perfect place to de-stress and think about ways to make lemonade out of her lemons.

Arthur Coley was waiting at the station in Camucia when Missouri stepped off the train. Over the phone before she left Florence, she offered to take the local bus up the mountain to Cortona. "Nonsense, Missouri. No need for you to wait for the bus when I can drive down to meet you in less than 10 minutes."

As they walked by seven people waiting at the bus stop, Missouri was glad Arthur had insisted on picking her up. She could feel her butt dragging. All she wanted to do was get to her room and collapse on her bed. Amelia would not approve, but she felt a "pity party" coming on.

Her art teacher's husband grabbed her duffle and tossed it in the back seat of an old black Fiat. "You will love Cortona, Missouri." He turned the key in the ignition and lowered his window. "Sorry, but the A/C died on this car several years ago."

Missouri fastened her seatbelt and looked in the distance at the walled city perched on the mountainside. "A/C? What's that? There certainly isn't any in our apartment in Florence or the studio either."

Arthur turned the car around in the station parking lot and headed towards Cortona. "Who needs it? Tuscany is definitely cooler and less humid than Georgia. You'll appreciate the cool breeze on the mountainside."

Missouri relaxed in the passenger seat and tried to let go of the tension she'd not been able to shake since David walked out of her life. In her mind, she kept re-playing all the events that occurred while Doyle and her sons were in

Florence. How could things have gone so badly downhill? What could she have done or said that would have made things end differently? Short of tying up Doyle and sending him back to Georgia in a shipping crate – absolutely nothing.

"Missouri?" She jumped as Arthur gently shook her shoulder. "You have to get out here. No cars beyond this point." Seconds after Arthur set Missouri's bag on the worn-out cobblestones, a middle-age Italian man stepped out of the shadows and grabbed it. "Missouri, this is Giorgio." Giorgio grunted. "He will take you to the *pensione* where you will be staying. I need to park the car, but I will see you at Tonino's for dinner at 7 o'clock."

Before Missouri could ask where Tonino's was, Arthur waved his hand at her and drove back down the cobblestone road. Missouri had no choice but to follow Giorgio and her bag up a steep narrow passageway between medieval buildings. "Come, *signora*, this way."

Omigosh, thought Missouri as she fell in line behind Giorgio. Were the people who lived in Cortona half mountain goats? She could not believe how steep the path was. Fortunately, for her, Giorgio stopped occasionally and waited for her to catch up. By the time she saw him open and enter through an ornate black gate, Missouri's lungs were burning, and she thought her heart was ready to burst in her chest.

As Missouri paused at the gate to catch her breath, she was surprised to see a beautiful small courtyard full of flowers. Giorgio dropped her duffle in front of an oak door, heavily carved with a floral design, and rushed past her and down the hill with only a departing grunt. Obviously a man of few words. When her breathing returned to normal, Missouri dragged herself to the door and knocked.

A teenage girl flung open the door. "*Si?*" Then she glanced down at Missouri's bag. Her eyes widened. "You are *Signora* Rothman, *si?*"

Missouri wiped the perspiration from her overheated face with a handkerchief. "*Si, io sono* Missouri Rothman."

The girl picked up Missouri's duffle bag and motioned her inside. "*Si prega di entrare. Vi aspettavamo.* We are happy to see you."

And if I don't pass out right here, thought Missouri, I will be happy, too.

• • • • •

Her room in the boarding house was small, but Missouri was pleased to see she would not be sharing it with anyone. Besides a single cot, the room contained an armoire for her clothes, a desk and chair, and a small sink. Toilet and shower were at the end of the hall and – according to Mama Lucia -- were shared with Marianne Karman from the University of Missouri.

By the time a knock sounded at her door around 6:45 p.m., Missouri had cooled her face with a damp cloth, put away her clothes and rested. "Good evening. Are you Missouri Rothman?" greeted a blonde-headed middle age woman. She reached out her hand to Missouri. "I'm Marianne Karman, and I'm teaching a summer class on Italian culture."

Missouri shook her hand and invited her into her room. "Good to meet you, Marianne."

"I'm here to walk you down to Tonino's for dinner." Marianne reached into her shirt pocket and handed her a folded piece of paper. "You will want this, trust me. It's a map of Cortona. This city is one huge maze. You will get lost often your first day or two."

Spreading out the map on the desk, Marianne produced a red pen and circled the *penzione*, Tonino's and the classroom/studio where Missouri would be teaching. "Mama Lucia cooks breakfast for us every morning. Lunch is wherever you can grab it, but the best place is the small supermarket on the Piazza della Repubblica. At Molesini they make the best *panini* sandwiches in town. Whatever you want. Then every evening, we get a full dinner at Tonino's."

Missouri followed Marianne down the hill. She tried not to think about walking back up the steep hill to the *penzione* after dinner. The hill leveled off in the Piazza della Repubblica. Marianne pointed out Molesini, which was across the piazza from the town hall, an imposing medieval building with a clock and bell tower and a wide stone staircase.

"Those steps look like they have been there since the beginning of time," Missouri said.

Marianne laughed. "You are close. It dates from the 13th century. This is one of two main squares. The people who live in Cortona gather here to socialize every day."

From the town hall, Marianne led Missouri down Via Nazionale, which to Missouri's relief, was flat. "Is this the main drag?" Missouri asked.

Marianne laughed, again. "Yes, that is exactly what it is. It goes all the way to Piazza Garibaldi, where the buses arrive throughout the day. I love to walk up and down this street and browse through the shops."

When the two women reached Piazza Garibaldi, Marianne guided Missouri to a wall with a breathtaking view of the valley below. As spectacular as it was,

Missouri thought it could not compare with the panoramic view of Florence from the Piazzale Michelangelo. She closed her eyes and remembered the day she first visited the square with David. Missouri, Missouri, Missouri! Stop torturing yourself. She turned away and followed Marianne into Tonino's.

· · · · ·

Arthur greeted Missouri and led her to an empty seat next to him. While everyone helped themselves to plates of antipasta already on the table, he introduced her and a young bearded man with shoulder-length brown hair – the summer semester photography instructor.

"Did you get settled into your room?" Arthur asked Missouri.

She swallowed a bite of *prosciutto* ham and melon. "Yes, thank you. I like not having to share a room."

"Yes, Thelma said you needed privacy and time to think." He winked and smiled.

The kitchen door opened and two waiters came out with plates of steaming *tortellini* in a garlic butter sauce. Missouri took a bite and blinked back the tears. It reminded her of David's pasta dishes. The main course -- whole poached salmon – was brought to the table on a long wooden board and served by the spoonful. This also reminded her of David. A lump rose in her throat. For goodness sakes, Missouri, will you get a grip? You're over half a century old! You're acting like a love-sick high school girl who was dumped by "Mr. Wonderful."

· · · · ·

Two weeks later, while Marianne and most of the instructors crowded into a coffee bar off the Repubblica square, Missouri excused herself, climbed halfway up the town hall steps and sat down to call Gabriella on her cell. She always used her WhatsApp to talk to Gabby and Cody, but she had not communicated with either Michael or Doyle since they left Florence. Missouri didn't want to deal with any disagreeable people.

Gabriella answered on the fourth ring. "Missouri, is that you?"

From the background noise, it was obvious to Missouri that Gabriella was having coffee with friends as usual. "I can barely hear you, Gabby."

"*Un moment, s'il vous plait.*" After a few seconds, the noise faded out. "How is this?"

"Yes, that's better, Gabby."

"*Maintenant*, Missouri, *s'il vous plait* – tell me how you are."

Missouri sighed. "I don't understand. Everything reminds me of David and I feel so weepy."

"You think you made a mistake leaving Florence?"

Missouri covered her face with her hand. "No. Maybe. I'm not sure. But I was drowning in Florence. I couldn't breathe. I had to leave." She paused. "Have you seen David?"

"You wonder if he misses you?"

"No, of course not. Do you think I care? I'm sure he hasn't even noticed my absence. Has he?" Missouri thought she heard a cross between a snort and a cackle.

"You crazy American woman! David actually sat down and had coffee with me tonight."

Missouri felt her pulse quicken. "Oh? Did he ask about me?"

"*Un moment.* Let me think. Did he?" Pause. "He may have asked if you returned to Georgia."

"What did you say?"

"No, of course."

"What did he say?"

"Nothing."

"Nothing?"

"Nothing."

Missouri banged her forehead on her knees. "That was it?"

"Then he said, 'Good night, Gabby,' and left."

Missouri gripped her cell phone so tight, her fingers hurt. "See? He doesn't care about me at all. He's moved on. I need to do the same." If only she could.

• • • • •

After her talk with Gabriella, Missouri tried even harder to put David out of her mind. She threw herself into her teaching. That was not hard to do. The eight students in her portrait class were talented and eager to learn about portraiture. She was surprised at how much she enjoyed teaching. Maybe she should consider getting a dual major with art education. Definitely something to think about. Art teachers did get paid for teaching. That would make Doyle happy.

Dang it! She didn't care about Doyle's happiness. Or even about Doyle period.

Outside of class, Missouri had plenty of time to think and paint the medieval buildings, Etruscan tombs, breathtaking landscapes of the valley below and portraits of the people who lived on this mountainside. Her favorite places to go to be alone with her thoughts and her watercolors were the *Basilica di Santa Margherita* and the *Fortezza Medicea di Girifalco* – both high up on the mountainside and outside of the medieval walled town of Cortona.

The last week of Missouri's portrait class, Arthur Coley stopped her as she was headed up the Via S. Margherita towards the Basilica with her watercolors. "Good afternoon, Missouri! How is your class going?"

Missouri shifted her stool to her left hand to shake hands with him. "Hello, Arthur! The class is going well, thank you. The students have their final critiques this Friday. Then we plan to have a farewell dinner at Trattoria Dardano."

He smiled and nodded. "Ah, yes. Your artist residency will be up the end of this week. Have you made plans for afterwards? Back to Florence or back to Georgia?"

Missouri sighed. "To be honest, I have put any decision-making out of my mind. Since I'll still have a few weeks before fall classes begin at the Academy, I was thinking of taking a few days to see the Amalfi Coast. Maybe visit Sorrento or the Isle of Capri."

Arthur placed his hand on Missouri's shoulder. "Sounds like a good plan, but make sure you let Thelma know what's going on. You know how much she cares about you and any decisions you make."

Missouri laughed at the thought of her former high school art teacher sitting by the phone, waiting on her to call and report in. No, Thelma would pick up the phone and call her first. "Don't worry, your wife will be the first person I'll call." Missouri gave Arthur a wave and began her climb up the steep hill. When she first arrived in Cortona, she had to stop five or six times to catch her breath before reaching the Basilica. Now she was able to get to the top without stopping once. Her body was in good shape; she just wasn't sure about the rest of herself.

•   •   •   •   •

"Looks like you're using a little too much burnt sienna. I'd go with some ultraviolet." The voice came from behind her. David's voice.

Missouri's hand holding the brush froze. Something deep inside tingled and quivered. "Thank you, but I like it just the way it is."

"You might be making a mistake." The voice was much closer now. "After all, I have many more years of painting experience than you."

Missouri put down her brush and turned around to face David, who stood only a foot away. She was half way through her last week in Cortona. In just days, she would have to leave this lovely, medieval-walled city and get on with the rest of her life. Whatever that would be. And there stood the man she could not get out of her mind. The man who dominated every thought and dream. She felt her heart racing. "Just because you're experienced doesn't necessarily mean you're always right," she responded without emotion.

"Yes, I know," he said softly, sitting down on the boulder beside her. A silence ensued between them.

Missouri picked up her brush, daubed at the burnt sienna and returned to her watercolor. How had he found her? She applied color to her landscape. And why was he here?

David contented himself with watching her work and enjoying the view of the valley down below. For nearly an hour she worked and neither said a word. Finally, Missouri rinsed out her brush and began packing up her watercolors, palette, paper and brushes.

David sighed. "I love it up here." He pointed to the valley below. "Look, there's the train arriving from Florence. Looks like a model railroad from here. You can almost see the sailboats on Lake Trasimeno. And don't you love how the patchwork of earth goes from farmland to poppy fields, villages and olive tree groves? I've yet to see any artist who could do it justice."

Missouri tucked her paint rags in her bag and zipped it up. Ready to start her descent down the mountain to Cortona, she turned to David and spoke softly. "Okay, Professor Harris, how did you know where to find me?"

David continued to look out over the valley below. "I am not without my resources. I called Thelma Coley because she wrote one of your letters of recommendation. Her letter was so glowing, I figured you had been in contact with her. I was right."

"That explains how you knew where I was, but why are you here? In Florence you made it perfectly clear that you did not want to have anything to do with me. Yet here you are."

David stood up to face Missouri and brushed off the seat of his cargo pants. "I just happened to come up for the great view. What a coincidence that you were up here painting," he said innocently.

Missouri hefted her painter's bag strap over her shoulder. "There's no way this meeting on a desolate mountaintop could be by chance," she said accusingly.

He looked down at his hiking boots. "No, I guess not." He took a step toward her, but she backed away from him. "Please, Missouri. I just want to talk to you."

Missouri shook her head and turned away. She could feel herself trembling. "I don't think so. You said enough to me last time." She started down the path toward Cortona.

David grabbed her arm. "Please, wait. Sit down and hear me out."

She paused and turned her head in his direction. "Why?"

"Because I'm young, witty, charming and good-looking, and you have a soft spot in your heart for talented artists."

Missouri rolled her eyes and continued walking at a fast clip. "Not good enough."

David ran along beside her. "How about because I'm a young, foolish, stupid man who has come to apologize for his boorish behavior?"

Missouri paused and looked at him. "You're sorry you ripped a knife into my heart and drove me away?"

"Yes." He took a step closer.

She backed away. "It's a little too late." She continued down the path. Even when she heard David at her heels, she didn't stop.

"Missouri, I only did it because your sons came to me and told me I was preventing you and Doyle from getting back together. That they wanted their family back."

Missouri did not slow her steps, but David stopped following her.

"I had to give you a chance to rekindle your love for your husband," he called after her. "I love you so much I was willing to let you go in hopes that you would find your way back to me...and marry me...even if I am a total jerk who doesn't deserve you and who has no expectations that you would ever forgive me much less marry me and be the wife of such an insensitive idiot, barely out of puberty." Missouri stopped her downward descent. It felt like all of her body heat was rising to her neck and face. She swallowed the lump that was forming in her throat and turned around. David was standing about 10 feet away. His head hung low, his shoulders sagged. Missouri ran back to him and grabbed him around the neck. The tears streamed down her face. He said he loved her. He wanted to marry her. His words echoed in her brain. "Yes, Professor Harris! Yes, I'll marry you."

He smiled. "Really? You will? You don't hate me?"

"Cody told me that he and Michael persuaded you to back away from me."

"Yes, that's true. I wanted to give you the freedom to decide what you wanted to do. I thought if I stepped away, it would be easier for you to make that decision."

"So kiss me before I change my mind. Who knows how much longer I have before senility and old age set in; we don't have any time to waste."

View other Black Rose Writing titles at www.blackrosewriting.com/books and use promo code PRINT to receive a 20% discount when purchasing.

BLACK ROSE writing™

CPSIA information can be obtained
at www.ICGtesting.com
Printed in the USA
BVHW031941140920
588796BV00001B/190